volume one

making a case for murder

doing what has to be done

lar e hale

For Colette,

It was a pleasure to meet you. Very nice dress!

Hope you enjoy.

Lar E Hale

Copyright 2017

ISBN-13: 978-1973965558
ISBN-10: 1973965550

This is a work of fiction. Characters and incidences are the product of the author's imagination and are used fictitiously.

Published August 2017 by lar e hale

acknowledgements

I'd like to thank my beta-reader, Jackie, who read the book as I wrote it, said she was 'hooked,' and asked me to continue sending new chapters.

I'd also like to thank JoAnna for her valuable insight, Jen for an endearing comment she uttered long ago, Tana for providing much-needed information, and Steve for being such an interesting guy as well as a damn good fisherman.

I'd especially like to thank my editor, who asked to remain nameless. She said some of the story was a little too graphic for her liking and didn't want to be associated with my ilk. She also happens to be my best friend, and her continued encouragement is the reason you're reading this. So, if you don't like the book, blame her.

That's what I'm going to do.

Books by Lar E Hale

The Murder Series

making a case for murder
doing what has to be done

when murder becomes mayhem
some people need to die

murder in the light of day
right and wrong are relative

let's begin

He'd been watching her for a while now.

She moved with grace and seemed much older at first glance, with an alluring smile and confident manner. The contour of her body was compelling, and his eyes caressed her long legs from calf to inner thigh. The buttons of her blouse strained against the fullness of her breasts, and her lips looked soft and inviting.

She was young. Too young, and he had no right.

But he'd take her all the same.

chapter one

I had that dream again.

After wiping the cobwebs from my eyes, I wondered about the origin of that expression and considered the tensile strength of a spider's web, the intrinsic beauty of its elegant design, and the reason for its construction.

To kill or not to kill?

That is the question, and, with apologies to the Bard for co-opting his words, I contemplated again the fullness of its meaning and the consequences of my actions.

Killing is not an easy thing.

Okay, sure, the act itself was simple enough – you shot, stabbed, bludgeoned, poisoned, strangled, blew the hell up. But could I live with it?

People killed all the time for all sorts of reasons: love, country, family, fear, race, religion, envy, jealousy, revenge, hate. For money or advantage.

For fun.

I began to formulate a plan, applying the who, what, where, when, why, and how standard of inquiry.

The *why* determined the *who,* and that person and reason had already been established. The *when* and *where* were dependent upon the how, and the *how* of killing would be the cornerstone of my success.

How did one effectively subdue someone else?

Or properly dress to prevent the transfer of DNA, surveil without being seen, acquire the necessary tools without raising suspicion, properly dispose of a body . . .

I couldn't just ask my friend if he happened to know the decomposition rate of a person buried in the woods using seasonal weather norms as a baseline measurement. He'd most likely mention it to someone at some time and might be a little nervous the next time we went hunting together.

Of course, that sort of information was available and accessed all the time – by students writing papers, authors needing material, historians wanting data, and others who were just plain curious. But internet activity is monitored, and libraries regularly flag books like Justin Thyme's, *So, You Want to Start Killing People* – which, by the way, has an excellent chapter on blood spatter patterns in the section entitled Hammers: Ball-peen vs Claw.

Suspicion was not an option. It led to observation, scrutiny, complication, and probable incarceration or death. So, in order to keep a low profile, I'd have to KISS it - keep it simple, stupid - and learn to rock as I rolled.

Procuring the tools and equipment should be a less risky proposition than asking Siri how to do this or that. Those items could be garnered by conventional means if I used cash, spread my purchases around, and bought critical items early as they would most likely be tracked later.

Shovels, axes, knives, gloves, rags, rope, zip-ties, and good old duct tape seemed part of the serial killer's basic starter kit and some of those things I already had, assuming my fingerprints and DNA residue were carefully eliminated. I also had something else.

Incentive, fused with urgency.

~~

Mary Stewart worked on a complex problem using equations invented by the ancient mathematician, Euclid. Her mind focused, she walked rather than skipped on the chalked outline of a hopscotch pattern, subconsciously avoiding the cracks in the sidewalk. A steady and persistent sound broke her concentration.

Watson.

"Hello to you, too," she said, moving her fingers behind his ears and smiling when he cocked his head.

Since junior high, the length of her school day had gotten longer and longer. They didn't play as often but still cared deeply for each other. Whenever she had a problem,

2

he'd listen, never interrupting. He was her best friend, and she gave him a hug and a kiss before she left.

Mary finished her homework: American history, English literature, Spanish and math. Lots of math.

She stretched the kinks from her neck and let the numbers bounce around in her head. Beautiful prime numbers, fractions dividing other fractions, strings of figures with decimal points – she loved them all.

Her teacher, Mrs. Hunter, recognized her affinity for numbers and formulae and encouraged her to participate in an online Advanced Mathematics Program offered by Florida State University. She became the youngest student in the quad-county area to be accepted.

A few people at her school thought it was a big deal. Like the principal, and the kids eating lunch at the nerd table. She did, too.

Spaghetti sauce and noodles were on the stove with some garlic bread on the counter waiting to go in the oven. A salad of Romaine lettuce, thinly sliced purple onions, olives, shredded cheese and ham sat covered in the fridge.

She practiced her pattern exercises while the noodles continued to boil. Her fingers flew over the guitar frets, and she closed her eyes as the fingertips found their place without hesitation or mistake. She'd been up and down the fretboard a few times when something banged against the house, startling her.

Mary looked out back and noticed the darkening sky. The wind tossed about the branches of an old oak tree, one she had climbed for years.

A storm was coming.

~~

I wanted to get into her house without being seen, but, because some people were now helping UPS and FedEx redeliver *our* packages to *their* houses, many homes now had security cameras. I needed to find them, as well as any dogs close enough to bark when I tried to gain entry.

How could I accomplish this?

3

Walking up and down the street taking pictures or mental notes would draw attention; however, I might get the information by placing a video camera on either side of the backseat windows and driving down the block.

The idea had merit but wasn't foolproof – my vehicle might be recorded on the very cameras I was trying to locate. It would help if I had a legitimate reason to be on her street. A garage sale, maybe? If so, I'd be just another car driving around the neighborhood.

Who knows, I might even find something useful. A hunting knife, perhaps. Or a nice crowbar.

~~

Watson took his usual walk around the front yard, catching up on the latest smells, exchanging pleasantries, and chatting with a couple of birds about the goings on in the neighborhood and beyond.

He'd like to venture out and see some of the sights but was careful to stay within the confines of the electronic boundary surrounding the property. Although it had been a long time since he'd crossed it, the pain from the shock collar still haunted his memory.

A squirrel went on and on about the bumper crop of acorns this year, how proficient he was at procuring them, and how smart he was in faking out the other squirrels by pretending to bury the nuts, then hiding them while they were busy digging and trying to steal what wasn't there.

Watson knew an abundance of acorns might be a precursor to a long, cold winter and thought to tell him, but his eyes glazed over as the squirrel bragged about an almost perfect circle he'd carved for the doorway of his treehouse.

The clanging of the garage door gave him a reprieve from the squirrel's incessant rambling. He turned his head and saw the man looking up and down the street with a strange expression on his face.

What is he doing?

As the garage door began its slow, downward journey, Watson looked at the man looking directly at him, and the hackles rose down the middle of his spine.

~~

4

He searched her room and found a good place to hide it, the air intake vent. It was high enough to prevent detection with wide slats for a full, unobstructed view.

The camera sat in the center for optimal coverage. He checked the wireless connectivity, moved the zoom in and out, and tested the audio feature, all from the screen on his tablet. The picture quality was excellent.

He knew he should stop, before it was too late.

But he didn't want to.

chapter two

Mary heard him barking as she got off the bus. "What are you going on about?"

When she squatted to scratch behind his ears, Watson opened his mouth to speak and then turned his head to the right, shaking his leg. He never ceased to be amazed at how she always found the spot. That one spot.

When they were pups, they'd spend all day together, playing, running, fetching, and scratching. As Mary grew older, she spent more time in school leaving less time for play. Lately, she'd been staying after for ukulele – or was it Euclidean? They'd been talking for years, but the subtleties of sound and syllable were sometimes still confusing.

Mary always stopped by for a scratch and greet on her way home. Sometimes they'd talk about the happenings in their lives, and sometimes they'd enjoy the pleasure of each other's company in blissful silence.

He loved her as if she'd come from the same litter – his sister from another mister.

Watson became aware of drool and tongue hanging from his mouth when she kissed his nose, jiggled his ears, and gave his head a couple of quick pats.

"Sorry, gotta go. Fetch ya later."

Still basking in the glow of her affection, he watched her walk across the street, up the steps, and into the house before remembering he'd forgotten.

"Wait. Mary. I need to tell you something . . ."

The door closed before she heard him.

~~

After brushing and flossing, Mary scrunched her nose while swishing the mouthwash a full minute before spitting into the sink.

"Eck."

She whooshed some water around and spit again.

"Euhhg."

Catching a glimpse of herself in the mirror, she laughed out loud, tired and getting goofy. She opened the door of the vanity and tossed the hair dryer onto the shelf under the sink. The expected bang as dryer hit shelf was followed by another, making her jump.

She kneeled and saw a piece of wood hanging. Something must have fallen through the splintered opening in the bottom of an unknown and unused drawer.

The vanity was counter and sink, with three drawers across and two doors below. Shelves were behind the doors, and the left and right drawers held a myriad of bathroom sundries. The middle one had never opened, and Mary had always assumed its purpose was aesthetic.

Intrigued, she pulled hard on the handle. It didn't budge. She looked around and found the fallen item, opened the black box and saw a shiny, silver something.

"What is this?"

A blush warmed her cheeks when it dawned on her. She wondered what else might be in the not-a-drawer drawer but was too tired to satisfy her curiosity. She left the box on the shelf under the sink, turned off the light, and heard the familiar squeak as she walked down the hallway to the quiet coziness of her room.

After closing the door, she let the towel drop to the floor and reached for the skin cream on the dresser, the lotion cool in her hand. She set the bottle down, rubbed her hands to warm the smooth liquid, and then slid them over her arms and shoulders and neck.

She closed her eyes, calm and relaxed.

A grin formed when she remembered putting her favorite sheets on the bed this morning, an Egyptian cotton birthday present with an eight-hundred thread count. Her hands moved to her breasts in anticipation of the smooth fabric against her skin, and she quivered. Mary's eyes opened, and, again, caught a glimpse of herself in the mirror.

Until a few months ago, she'd never given much thought to how she looked. She had her math, her music, and boys were just boys. Then... she started to develop. *Over-develop is more like it.*

When she'd returned to school after summer vacation, the girls either ignored her or made snide comments, and the boys looked at her in a different way and rarely in the eyes. Even some teachers would stare.

She'd tried hiding her breasts under blouses way too big, hoping to deflect the derision and unwanted attention of her classmates, but the whistles and unkind remarks continued.

One day, some girls giggled behind her, and when she turned around, they stopped and looked away. It didn't upset her, but she didn't feel good about it.

When the bell rang, Mrs. Hunter asked her to stay for a minute. Someone said, "Teacher's pet," and one of her friends snickered. Mary started to say something but didn't.

"Don't pay them any mind," Mrs. Hunter said when they were alone. "Most of those girls are a bit jealous, is all."

"Why would they be jealous of me?"

"Well, you're smarter than them, and they don't like it. Nothing can be done about that."

She paused for a moment, knowing she could get into trouble. It wasn't school policy to talk with students about personal issues, but she cared about Mary and didn't want to see her confidence diminished.

"You're also bustier than them, and they don't like it." She smiled. "Nothing can be done about *that*, either."

"I try to cover-up, to keep hidden, but . . ."

"Sweet girl. When God gave you a bosom, He gave with both hands, that's for sure. But like a candle, He doesn't want you to hide your bosom under a basket. You need to be who you are, or else who *are* you? Be proud, stand tall, and don't let those girls bother you. Their day, and their bosoms, will come."

She'd understood what Mrs. Hunter told her, remembering the story from vacation bible school.

'Don't hide your candle under a bushel basket but place it on a stand for all to see.'

Mary stared at the girl in the mirror, admiring the way her breasts contrasted with the small waist, and how the contour of her hips flowed seamlessly to sculpted legs. When she smiled, the girl did the same.

She let a hand drift from her breast to her stomach. Touch was nice. It called and haunted, pleased and excited. It satisfied.

Someone at school was pregnant.

What had she been thinking? That girl wasn't thinking, she was feeling. *Or, more likely, being felt.*

Mary chuckled at her little joke.

She was curious too, just like that girl, and wondered what it would feel like to be with someone. What teenage girl didn't think about it? But Mary had plans for college and travel that didn't include having a baby, especially at such a young age. No way would she squander the opportunity to learn all there was to know, and experience everything the world had to offer an unencumbered young woman in the prime of life. That's why she wouldn't be having sex with anyone for a long time.

Well, except with herself.

One of the effects of developing so quickly was she tended to *feel* the change. The elevated hormone levels made her body acutely responsive to touch, and she'd explored herself completely, moving from curiosity and titillation, to sensuality and desire.

She didn't feel shame or suffer any guilt. This was her choice, her body, and her business. It was personal and private. It belonged to *her*.

Mary got into bed and turned off the light. As the silky Egyptian cotton caressed her, she thought about the black, textured box, and the silver something inside of it.

She cupped her breast, her fingers tracing circles round and around. When they wandered to the warmth of her white panties, her lips parted.

~~

It was the moan that did him in.

Her naked body was everything he imagined it would be. The paradox of her innocence and experience was mesmerizing, and he saw the unabashed satisfaction she derived from touching herself.

The expression on her face was exquisite as she sought her climax with patience and determination, and he trembled with exhilaration when she found it. Her orgasm was an irresistible force, but that moan . . .

It wasn't loud. In fact, you wouldn't have heard it unless you were in the room. It came from within, deep from within, and sang like a siren's song. It beckoned to him, calling out as certainly as if she had spoken the words.

Take me.

chapter three

I estimated my chances of success at around ninety-two percent, and my level of confidence was relative. I felt rushed, and I was, wishing there was more time to plan.

But I couldn't wait.

The images from the video burned my heart and mind as I watched her fingers move with dexterity and purpose, creating a sound that was music to my ears.

I had to do it. I *needed* to do it.

Tonight.

~~

She was flying.

It came easily to her. Sometimes, she'd run and jump into the air. Other times, she would stand with outstretched arms at her side and rise.

Mary only flew at night - not too far and not for long. Once she rose straight up, reached out and touched the face of space. It was glorious! She'd laughed and fell to earth, watching the stars wink at her as she winked back.

She yawned and considered home and bed but flew to the forest, drawn to the moonlit darkness of the woods.

Careful to avoid the creak, he crept down the hall, heart pounding in anticipation. He didn't have a single thought about stopping what he was doing, but plenty about what he was going to do.

His hand trembled as he turned the knob.

She lay on the lush forest floor and gazed above the treetops at the night sky filled with countless stars.

The balmy breeze swept over her skin and she closed her eyes, letting it touch her. She moaned when the wind licked, creating a gust. The sensation, new and unexpected, ignited her passion. The emerging whirlwind began to overwhelm her senses and continued to swirl in intensity until her body erupted and convulsed.

Mary had never experienced such a powerful orgasm and was in a state of ecstasy that left an indelible mark on her psyche. When her breathing slowed, she opened her eyes to starless dark and Egyptian cotton.

It had all been a dream. A wet dream, her first. She started to grin but stopped when the wind reached for her.

"No . . ."

A smelly rag covered her face, making her weak and sleepy. She tried to fly away but couldn't raise her arms.

Watson let out a low whine.

He'd seen her high above, but she hadn't seen him. When Mary flew to the forest, he followed after her. Halfway to the woods he started to run faster and faster. Something was wrong!

Someone was hurting her, taking her.

Yvette looked over at Watson lying in his bed, eyes closed and feet moving in the air.

~~

She was bound, gagged, drunk, and drugged.

He'd threatened to kill her if she screamed or made any attempt to escape, but the only time he'd hurt her was the first time he took her.

And now?

When she struggled, it only amplified his arousal, and if she laid still, hoping to dampen his desire, he'd delight in trying to overcome her reticence.

Mary wished he'd just take her in painful, violent ways, because what he was doing, and the way he was doing it, was pure evil. He knew things he shouldn't, private things, and . . .

She felt debased and deeply ashamed. How could she ever face anyone again? She hated him.

She hated herself.

The tears burned as they rolled down her cheeks, and Mary withdrew into the solitude of her soul.

~~

She wanted it, he was sure, but couldn't admit it to herself. And that conflict fed his voracious appetite.

He'd heard her true feelings, expressed under protest, but the *song* was muted because of the gag. While necessary to keep her from shouting for help, he ached to know what that moan felt like unfettered and reverberating in his ear.

A shiver of excitement ran through him as he resolved to hear it at least once before he killed her.

~~

Watson tried to go after her the moment the front door opened, but the shock from the collar put him on the ground when he crossed the edge of the grass. He howled in pain and had to crawl back to find relief behind the boundary.

When Yvette ran outside, he told her about Mary, but she didn't understand and restricted him to the fenced-in back yard. Whenever he tried to tell anyone about the trouble his friend was in, Yvette made him come in the house. She wouldn't let him out at night anymore, saying his *barking* was aggravating the neighbors and threatening him with a visit to the vet.

Today, he'd try a different tactic. As soon as his feet hit the back yard, he'd play with his ball. He'd throw it and chase it and appear to have a grand old time. When Yvette moved from the window, he'd toss it by the corner of the house. Little by little, he'd dig behind the hedge until he could crawl under the fence and try, again, to go to Mary.

He didn't think Yvette would catch on. She was reasonably intelligent by human standards but, she was no Golden Retriever.

~~

An owl asked *who*, but I didn't respond. It's a big forest and he may not be talking to me. The sliver of moon was dim enough to appreciate the grandeur of the galaxy and bright enough to finish my work. It only took fifteen-plus minutes to fill a hole that had taken almost an hour to dig.

A shooting star crossed the night sky as I examined the ground one last time. It should go unnoticed and unfound, assuring what had been done to her would stay unknown.

To avoid creating a path by walking the same way out of the woods, I headed toward the lane along a different route. As I neared the edge of the forest I stopped, listened, and looked. There it was, right where I'd left it.

Not wanting to leave evidence from the gravesite inside the vehicle, I changed clothes, shoes, and gloves before stowing the soiled items in a throwaway bag. After putting on a new pair of latex, I unscrewed the shovel blade from the handle, intending to toss both miles apart.

The air smelled of pine as I drove down the lane and listened to the night, reminded of a dark and lovely verse. I'd had a long and busy day and looked forward to shower and bed – but I had miles to go before I slept.

I thought about the question I'd asked myself earlier. Can I live with it?

Yes. I can.

chapter four

There are two sections of Stevie Ray Vaughan's version of the Jimi Hendrix song, *Little Wing*, I can't play correctly to save my life. It didn't come naturally to me, or, more to the point, immediately. I'd end up playing my own version, and, though the people seemed to like it, an accurate rendition it was not.

But honestly, I didn't put in the time to get it right. I'd learn just enough to play in front of people with a modicum of confidence and move on to the next song. And the *people* I liked to play for were those who drank and talked and didn't pay much attention to me. That's my crowd.

I played the section that gave me the most fits, slower this time, and got almost to the end without a single mistake when the door knocked.

Shoot!

I started over. Another knock.

Damn it.

Now, I don't usually feel an obligation to answer a door or a phone. Just because someone wanted to talk to me, didn't mean I wanted to listen. But I was in a guitar playing mood with a paying gig tonight, so, if I wanted to practice, I needed to move the distraction down the road.

Hmmm. They looked official.

"Hi. I'm Detective Williams, and this is my partner, Detective Greer. We're from the St. Vincent PD. Are you Dax Palmer?"

Before I said a word, the incredible speed and processing power of the human brain had already analyzed and collated a few things and invited me to consider them.

How did a person who'd killed someone behave versus one who hadn't in relation to body language, eye contact, demeanor? This should be interesting.

"Yes. How can I help you?"

I thought about inviting them in but decided against it. There were too many variables with too many outcomes. For example, if one of them tried to open a door, it would require a response of some kind. Even a non-response could be construed as suspicious behavior.

Better to avoid the risk altogether.

"May we come in?"

Now that's funny. I opened the door and stopped.

"Uh, maybe not. It's not a total mess, but it's more than I'm comfortable sharing."

I left the door open for another three seconds before joining them on the porch. Seven or eight seconds while I told them *maybe not,* plus three more, gave them a good ten seconds to look behind and around me, which they did. Finally, a tangible benefit to being so casual about cleaning. I'm not a slob by any means, but sometimes . . .

When Detective Greer didn't say anything, I looked over to Detective Williams, who seemed to be in charge. She had a pair of remarkable eyes, hazel-green with gold flecks. They were not only beautiful, but conveyed intelligence. A slight smile lit on her face.

How long had she seen me seeing her?

"Do you own a mini-van? A Dodge Grand Caravan?"

I guess Greer had something to say after all. Was that a trace of disdain in his voice? Like I was a soccer mom? I used that van to transport things. All kinds of things.

"Yes, I do."

"Can we see it?" asked Williams.

Interesting. One asked a question, while the other observed. It was probably just standard procedure, part of their training. I looked her in the eye. The left one, actually.

"I don't mind showing you, if you'll tell me why, first."

I saw Greer's expression change out of my periphery and imagined the police just wanted to be answered in the affirmative, without dissent or delay, whether they had a right to it or not.

Maybe he thought I was being a smartass? A friend of mine says I have a *tone* that comes through loud and clear sometimes. I hadn't meant to irk him. Detective Williams, on the other hand, didn't appear irked at all.

"I don't mind telling you, if you'll show it to us, first."

She had a sparkle in her eyes, and I thought she might be having a little fun in an otherwise boring day. I pulled out a quarter and raised my eyebrow.

An involuntary smile leapt to her face, and I swore the wattage in those eyes increased.

After losing the toss, I reached inside the front door and pushed the button on the extra remote. As we walked to the garage, I thought I might gain some insight into what they knew or suspected based on how they looked over the van.

Williams took a pen from her pocket to write down the license plate number, and Greer walked up the side of the van to the front. I liked how they'd split up and appreciated how this might be useful. While a suspect watched one detective, the other could look for tension, distress, or fear.

I didn't know if they were employing this tactic, but I stood to the left and behind - just in case.

Greer did a cursory visual of the vehicle, not looking at anything in particular, and I glanced over to Detective Williams, who was watching me. She returned my smile.

They didn't examine the tire tread or ask to look inside. It could mean I had nothing to worry about. Or, they didn't want to tip their hand before coming back with a warrant.

"Do you want the long reason why or the short one?" she asked as we walked back to the porch.

If I *was* a suspect, wouldn't I want to know as much as possible? "The short version is fine."

Unless she was good at keeping her thoughts hidden, I didn't see anything in her riveting, flecked eyes suggesting she suspected me of anything.

Those eyes . . .

They held my attention for too long, because I should have observed Greer's reaction as well. Those damned eyes. They were starting to look like trouble.

"We're tying up some loose ends on an old case," she said. "There are over seven thousand vehicles like yours throughout the state, and we're trying to account for them. Well, Detective Greer and I are only tracking down those within a sixty-mile radius, which is fifty-three, if you can believe it. Yours is number seventeen."

My brain suggested something else for me to consider. After doing so, I declined to take the possible bait by asking, *What case?*

"Well, good luck with it then. Y'all take care and have a good day," I said and went inside, retrieved a Dr. Pepper from the fridge, and sat in the big chair.

"Did you hear any of that?"

"Yup."

"They may come back."

"I don't care. I'm not leaving you."

I looked over and nodded.

Mary was dead serious.

In the depths of her despair, she'd found a way. It was a sickening way, but her spirit had almost been broken. Even if she escaped, Mary didn't think she could live with what he'd done to her – or what she'd had to do. Her face flushed with shame, and she wanted to die.

But she didn't want him to kill her.

He removed the gag and the restraints after she *gave in*, and within a couple of days, she was allowed to walk around the house. He was there, of course. Always. Watching her.

Mary didn't give him any reason to doubt what she said or did, and what she did convinced him she belonged to him. At least she hoped so, because she was near the end of her.

He'd be working tonight and wouldn't return for hours, leaving her alone for the first time since she'd been free to move about. Suddenly, she began to panic.

What if he ties me up again before he goes?

Mary walked over to him, resting her head on his chest and then a hand behind his head as he kissed her neck. She groaned when he squeezed her bottom.

"Wake me when you get home."

"You know I will."

He let her go, grabbed his keys, and walked down the hall to a side door that opened to the garage.

She peeked through the closed drapes when the engine turned over and the garage door opened and held her breath, waiting for him to drive away and out of her life. Finally, he rolled down the driveway and left.

Mary raced to her room, threw a few things into a backpack, and put on some running shoes, deeply conflicted about her need to tell someone what he'd done, and her desperate fear of what she'd had to do being known.

Mrs. Hunter . . .

She'd know what to do and how to help her.

A chime Mary recognized as a text message sounded. She hadn't seen her phone since he took her. Another chime came from the kitchen, and she found it at the back of a cupboard above the refrigerator.

The messages were from him!

Her hands shook as she tapped the screen.

'At first, when you asked me to come and take you, I tried to resist. But you wore me down, and I'm glad you did. Now, I look forward to our time together.'

Mary was stunned and scrolled to read the second one.

'I didn't know you were making videos. Why would you do that? I deleted the ones I found on your phone, before anyone saw them. You don't want that, do you?'

She knew the meaning of those messages.

If she told anyone, he'd claim it was her idea and show what she'd been doing over the last few days as proof. Everyone would think she'd planned it, she'd wanted it. They wouldn't know the truth or believe it.

And if she didn't tell, he'd keep her there, keep touching her. Keep wanting her to . . .

No one could help her now. No one at all. She sat down with her desolation and wept.

Hours later, she stood and went to his room. On her way to the back door, she instinctively picked up the phone and stuck it in her pocket. Her eyes teared up when she thought of Watson. He would miss her. She said a silent goodbye to her friend and slipped out into the darkness.

Mary no longer wanted to die.

She *needed* to.

~~

Mary... No!

Watson woke with a start and began to whine. He'd heard her goodbye and felt her sorrow.

"What is it, boy? What's wrong?" Yvette asked, concern in her voice. He told her Mary was in trouble, that he needed to find her before it was too late.

"Stop barking so loud. I don't know what's the matter."

He tried to calm down so he could explain, help her understand. Mary was going away; she was leaving him.

Forever

Yvette held onto his collar and led him down the hall.

"Be quiet, Watson. I mean it. We're going to the vet first thing in the morning. I know something's wrong, but I don't know what. Please, be quiet. It's late, and the neighbors are sleeping. Please."

She opened the door and gently pushed his bottom with her foot. "I'll let you out in the morning, okay?"

He walked down the steps, finding it difficult to compose himself enough to think of how to find Mary in time. He was so afraid for her.

Watson looked around and saw his only way out. He might be able to squeeze through the small space but, even if he could jump that high, the windows were not recessed enough to give him anything to hold on to.

Seven pieces of rope with knotted ends hung from the ceiling, one about two feet from the wall and six or seven inches to the right of an open window. Yvette used the ropes to hang plants she germinated over the winter.

He pushed the volleyball into position and balanced his back feet on top of it, counted to three and jumped, catching the knotted rope with his teeth.

After waiting for gravity and friction to slow his swing, he brought his hind legs to his chest and kicked at the screen, creating a tear to pull himself through. He used feet, knees and legs to pull himself backwards through the window, inching his way to freedom until he could let go of the rope. The cool air felt good on his snout and he grinned.

Let's see the dogs at the Westminster show do that!

chapter five months ago

A five mile stretch of road sliced through the forest with a dirt lane cut in every mile or so – some a half-mile long. I drove it back and forth from Scallop Cove: a local bar, restaurant and general hangout. The drinks were good, the food was better, and the hanging out could be fun.

I'd been playing at the bar for about three months, blues, mostly, with some Hendrix, Santana, ZZ Top, Trower, and Van Halen thrown in. I wasn't great, but I wasn't terrible. You might even find yourself tapping a foot.

Tonight had been a good one at the Cove. On the way home, I thought about the mix of people who danced, people who talked, and people who drank. It was quiet enough to talk without yelling, but loud enough to cover my mistakes. A win-win situation.

The high beams caught something moving up ahead, probably a deer, and I slowed down following the *rule of three* – whenever one deer crossed a dark and lonely road, two more were sure to follow.

Except, that wasn't a deer.

I stopped and peered through the trees. Someone seemed to be walking down a dirt lane. I backed up, turned on the narrow path, and a flash of light reflected on my left. The shadowed silhouette behind the tree looked feminine, and I glanced around before shutting off the motor.

She didn't move.

"I'm not going to hurt you."

Nothing.

"Are you okay? Do you need help?"

Crickets chirped. Literally.

"I'm getting out, but I'm not coming in. I'm just going to stretch my legs. Okay?"

Moonlight cast a glow through the trees and lit her troubled face. The pain in her eyes was palpable, and I wanted to share it, to relieve her of some of its burden.

Was that even possible?

The tears of her anguish began to spill, and I couldn't think of any words to ease a pain that profound. Platitudes would have been an insult. We stood looking into each other for a long time as everything around us grew still ... until a noise made us jump.

She reached into her pocket and came out with a phone, letting loose a scream. I followed its arc when she threw it, watched it glance off a tree and hit the ground. When I turned my head toward her, she'd removed her backpack and pulled something from inside.

"No!"

I rushed forward, knocking her down. The sound of the gunshot reverberated off the trees into the night. I got up, but she didn't move.

Was she breathing? *Yes.*

Shot? *No.*

Knocked out? *Could be.*

Her pulse was good and her breathing steady. I put the backpack, gun, and phone in the van, muting the volume when a call from *Dad* came through.

I wasn't comfortable leaving her with anyone right now – even her father. After deleting a tracking app and disabling location services, I turned off the phone.

Until I had a better understanding of what was going on, she wouldn't be easy to find.

I found a lump on the back of her head when I laid her on the couch. She looked peaceful; her face free of the tension I'd seen in the forest.

She was, what - fourteen, fifteen? What problem, at such a young age, could only be solved by suicide?

Pregnancy, bullying, drugs, ridicule, loneliness ... kids dealt with so much adversity these days. I understood the pressures, but wished they'd wait until their brains were fully developed before opting out. I'm not against suicide in general, I just wanted teenagers to have the capacity to analyze and *think* to help counter how they *feel*.

What to do?

Given how she'd reacted, the phone seemed a good place to start. I grabbed a Faygo Rock and Rye and went outside to sit on the back porch, turning the Rattan chair so I could see her through the window.

While her phone powered up, I hummed a few bars from a song I'd played tonight. I didn't just play it well, I nailed it, especially the solo. I'd expected the bar to erupt in thunderous applause, but only five people clapped – two of them just playing a hand slapping game, not paying any attention to me at all. I thanked them anyway. One man's slapping game is another man's applause.

I considered contacting *Dad*. He'd called a few times and might be worried about her. Maybe she'd done this before? I tried to access her voicemail for messages, but it was password protected. He'd also sent a few texts – two before the calls and three after.

Hmmm.

The last three showed a worried father anxious to find his daughter, concerned about what she might be doing and with whom. But the ones sent earlier were bothersome.

Something was going on between them, and it troubled me. I glanced up at that little girl face and remembered how desperate it had looked from behind the tree.

I tapped the Gallery icon and searched for the kind of video the text alluded to, but none of the thumbnail pictures looked provocative. I also tapped the My Files icon, Device storage, and SD card, looking for any file or folder name that looked questionable. I didn't find anything.

Maybe he'd deleted them like the text said?

For the heck of it, I tapped SEARCH and typed Dad. Two videos popped up, *Daddy1* and *Daddy12*. They were the only videos in a folder nested inside the Android folder.

That piqued my curiosity and fed my suspicion.

If she'd been actively recording them, why would she hide them from herself on her own phone in a system folder? And if she *did* hide them, wouldn't they be together in one place, so when he deleted them they'd all be gone?

One of the video thumbnails appeared greenish, the other a flower decal against a white backdrop.

I played *Daddy1*.

It was recorded using some night-vision optics, which explained the greenish color. A man caressed a woman, who started to writhe. After she had a vigorous orgasm, the woman raised her head and looked at the man. The end.

Wait, that's not a woman. I stared at the girl on my couch. Was that her? The second video confirmed it.

She was having sex with her father.

The flower disappeared when she sat upright and began to move her hips with his hands on her breasts. Maybe she had set out to seduce him and record what they were doing like the text implied? Before long, she got on her hands and knees, lowering her head as he reached for her.

I'd seen enough and started to tap close when she lifted her face and looked at me, her countenance a reflection of her soul. The truth was in her eyes, and they spoke to me as clearly as they had in the woods. With every thrust, I saw her light dim and her spirit crumble.

She was being destroyed.

Her eyes locked onto mine when I tapped pause, and I couldn't look away. It would have been tantamount to abandonment. I thought about all she must have endured and felt the hopelessness of her reality.

It broke my heart.

A coyote howled, an owl hooted, and a raindrop fell onto the screen. And then another. I lifted my head and stared out into the night. The wind touched the tears on my face, and I turned to look at her through the window.

She was sitting up on the couch, looking at me, too.

I set a bottle of aspirin and a glass of water on the coffee table, the clinking of ice the only sound in the room. I went back to the kitchen, poured some Coke into another ice-filled glass and lingered, giving her time to collect herself without a stranger watching.

Funny, she didn't feel like a stranger to *me* anymore. Without any proof or corroboration, I'd turned speculation into fact. I believed what I'd seen in her eyes, on the phone, and in the forest.

I walked into the big room and sat in my favorite chair - an oversized, reclining, swiveling, rocker kind of thing, whose cushion was permanently indented with an imprint of my behind. After swiveling to the right, but keeping her in my periphery view, I started to rock as she watched me.

After a swallow of Coke, I hummed the song I'd played so well tonight. The one I'd killed. Why can't I kill them all? I stepped aboard a different train of thought to ponder that.

Her head moved as she looked around the room, stopping for a moment before turning back to me. She took a couple of aspirin from the bottle, washed them down, and took another, longer drink.

I turned and raised my glass, tipping it in a toast-like manner, still rocking and humming.

She looked at me for five, six seconds before tipping her own. I re-swiveled and kept my side-eye on her as she brought the glass to her mouth and emptied it. I told her water and other drinkables were inside the refrigerator. Four seconds later, she left the room and I continued to ride the *why can't I kill them all* express.

She returned and put a coaster under the glass before wrapping the afghan around her shoulders and sitting on the couch with her Mountain Dew.

Where had that coaster come from?

She nestled against the big, puffy arm and raised her glass. I smiled, and she returned a hint of her own. We sat for a long time – me rocking, her snuggling – and enjoyed the quiet while we sipped our sodas. I felt a calmness come over her. Don't ask me how, but I did.

"You play the guitar," she said, a statement rather than a question.

I nodded. "You?"

"Yup."

More rocking, more snuggling.

"You any good?"

"Yup," she said again.

I grinned. I liked a girl with confidence.

"You?"

She also had an economy with words. I liked that, too.

"I'm alright," I said.

Two and a half rocks later, she said, "Sure 'bout that?"

I cracked up, and her face softened as a trace of a twinkle appeared in her eyes. We looked at each other for a few minutes, and the connection I'd felt in the forest was affirmed. When she yawned, I took a deep breath.

"You can leave if you want, and I'll take you wherever you want to go. But I'd like you to stay, if you can, and get some rest." She looked away but didn't say anything.

"You're safe here. No one can find you. And no one is going to hurt you anymore."

I left to get pillows, sheets, blankets, and a couple of tee shirts, half expecting her to run out the door. If she did leave, it would be without the gun. And her phone, at least for now. He might call or leave another text, and I wanted more information about *Dad* before talking to the police.

With my arms full, I walked down the hallway to the living room but stopped before reaching the end. Her glass stood on the coaster, and the afghan lay in a bundle on the couch, but she was gone.

I couldn't believe how hard it hit me.

And then the sweet voice of an acoustic guitar drew me into the room. I don't know if she recognized my relief, but I put the bedding on the couch and walked to my bedroom. "See you in the morning."

The music stopped. One second. Two seconds.

"Night," she said, and then the music started up again.

Shadows from the fan danced across the ceiling as I lay listening to her play. Her fingering was impressive and her sense of timing just about perfect. She was good. Damned good. Better than me.

The little shit.

I rolled on my side, folded a pillow under my head, and thought about her suffering. And the need for it to end. It was curious I'd found her, given the conflict of conscience I'd been having about the unrelenting evil in the world.

I couldn't keep turning away from the agony of others, couldn't keep changing the channel like I'd do when Sara McLachlan sang in the background while abused animals peered into my soul.

Sending money didn't address the real problem though, did it? Am I wrong to think the owner of that beaten and malnourished dog needed to be held more accountable?

A battle in the war of my will was being fought daily, culminating in the recurring dream I'd been having.

A nightmare, really.

The nocturnal seed had been planted after watching a television documentary centered around the apprehension of men who'd blatantly, and with enjoyment, shot and killed unarmed people floating in the waters of the open sea.

In searching for those involved, the show's producer spoke with a former fisherman who'd witnessed the abuse and murder of people held hostage at sea – people being ransomed for their freedom even though they had already paid outrageous sums of money to board that very ship thinking they were being taken to safety.

The casual way he described how they were raped and beaten, butchered and thrown overboard had a profound effect on me. His laughter haunted me still.

That laugh . . .

He wasn't just a witness; he was a participant who indulged in the pleasure of human suffering. I could kill him, and everyone like him.

And there it was. The answer to the question that had plagued me for weeks – what could *I* do about the atrocities inflicted upon the innocent?

The need to do something had burned inside of me for a long time, and I began to think about what had to be done. About *doing* what had to be done.

"Sorry. I, uh . . ."

"Bathroom's down the hall, last door on the left."

"Thanks," she said and closed the door.

I didn't believe in fate, or destiny, or a God that answered prayers – that was silliness. But the symmetry of her need and mine gave me pause.

Why *can't* I kill them all?

chapter six

Mary moved slowly at first then faster as she began to sink. She was caught in a vortex and every revolution pulled her further into the blackened center. Regardless of how hard she tried, she couldn't halt the downward progression. She was going to drown and nothing could stop it.

She had given up.

A hand reached out. All she had to do was take it, but it seemed too late and too far away. And then she looked up – and saw he cared about her.

Mary was going under when she grabbed and held on as he pulled her out of the dream. She took a deep breath, opened her eyes, and looked around the room.

It was dark, and nothing was familiar. Everything was different and unknown.

She was home.

~~

Watson watched her being pulled from the vortex, and his sleeping eyes filled with tears as relief fell over him like a cool waterfall. He'd come a long way to find her . . .

After climbing out of the basement window, he'd stood at the electronic boundary summoning all his courage, knowing it would hurt. If he yelped or whined, someone would hear and try to stop him. He looked up at Sirius, the dog star, in the constellation Canis Major.

Wish me luck.

He backed up a few feet to get a running start, hoping to outrun what he knew he couldn't. The shock knocked him to the pavement, and he gritted his teeth and walked across the street to Mary's house.

He picked up the scent of her despair and followed it out of the neighborhood, limping, then crawling in agony.

The pain was unbearable as he put one paw in front of the other. When it finally stopped, Watson thought he'd died and crossed over to doggie heaven – until he saw the vehicle bearing down on him.

He jumped clear just before it swerved to miss.

The irony of crawling to that exact spot and being killed after almost dying to get there was not lost on him. He shook his head, vowing to speak to Yvette about getting a collar with a shorter radius and less shock intensity.

He pressed on with the smell of Mary in his nostrils and the ache of her sorrow in his heart. A faint whiff of her was in the air straight ahead, but he followed the scent on the ground to the right where the trees lined both sides of the road. After turning down a dirt lane, he stopped at a tree on the left. Her anguish and desperation saturated the area.

Watson had laid down and cried for his friend, until he fell asleep from exhaustion and found her in his dream.

~~

Blood, urine, feces, and vomit sloshed around, making it difficult to walk or even move about without slipping. But the hacking didn't stop. The screams of the others were muted for fear the carnage would be directed at them. All they could do was look away and cry. One more whack, and the arm fell into the water. There was laughter, malevolent laughter, and I woke up.

Behind closed eyelids, the images continued to flicker like a matinee movie. A profound pleasure, even joy, resonated in that laughter. The sound swirled around my mind and filtered down to my soul.

I wondered if those who dropped bombs on civilians, used chemical weapons on their own people, left explosives on the street, or fired semi-automatic weapons into sidewalk cafes shared the same twisted joyfulness.

Possibly, but I'd bet the people who laughed that way preferred a more hands-on approach. The tactile delight must be a thrilling aspect in finding their bliss.

Like raping your daughter.

I wiped the cobwebs from my eyes and thought about a spider's web, its strength and beauty, the complexities and symmetries, the way each strand intertwined, and how the slightest movement could be sensed regardless of the distance. Just as a spider in the center can feel a fly moving on the outskirts of a web, an act of inhumanity can be felt by others over thousands of miles.

Or only a few feet away.

I extrapolated and saw a similarity in the effect a single negative element had on the whole. A bad apple rotting the whole bushel sort of thing.

To kill or not to kill?

Can I justify it?

The question required me to consider a salient point. Is death a fair and proper punishment for rape?

The violation of a person's body also injured the mind and spirit. The damage wasn't a measurable thing, constant across the spectrum of experience; it affected different people in different ways and to different degrees.

Most were forever changed; however, and the quality of their lives permanently altered. The people they used to be were murdered as surely as if they'd been put into the ground and buried, the victims forced to live as diminished facsimiles of themselves.

Was it right they should suffer such life changing consequences while their assailants did not? Why should a murderer of innocent lives be allowed to live at all?

I considered the legal alternative but didn't have faith. Prosecutors would charge him for rape and molestation, but he might only be given a slap on the wrist if videos of her participation were presented as evidence.

She would be humiliated if people saw them, and they would because those videos would eventually find their way to the internet. Where could she ever go to escape the prurient interests of those who wanted to *see*?

There wouldn't be any justice for her, and she'd be back in that forest while her *Dad* went on with his life, uncaring and unrepentant for the harm he'd caused and the murder he'd committed.

Can I live with it?

After getting up and getting dressed, I opened the door to a smorgasbord of smells wafting down the hallway. Eggs, bacon, pancakes . . . Ham?

She was running up and down the fretboard doing some finger exercises, and she was doing them fast and easy. I couldn't help but smile knowing I'd never be as good. Not without starting all over with a guitar in my hands as a child. Maybe not even then.

She wore clothes she must have had in the backpack. Her hair hung behind one ear, and a small crease of concentration showed on her forehead. She was a cutie.

"Hey."

"Hey. There's breakfast."

She kept practicing, as I headed into the kitchen and took a bite of eggs. The texture was perfect and the taste? *Oh, yeah.*

I grabbed a Mountain Dew from the fridge, walked into the room, and put my breakfast bonanza on the table.

"Use a placemat."

"What? Where . . ."

A couple sat on the shelf below the coffee table. I set my plate on a mat and the soda next to it.

"Coaster."

I shook my head and got one from the shelf while the needle on my like-o-meter began to twitch.

Chewing on a piece of bacon, I began to formulate a plan. I had an idea about a certain aspect of a specific task and picked up yesterday's copy of the St. Vincent Gazette from the shelf. Two garage sales were near her house.

I finished eating and swiveled the chair around to watch her. Something was different. *She* was different. She was - lighter. A full-on twinkle shined in her eyes.

She loved to play.

With her fingers on the twelfth fret, she began a downward progression at a blistering pace using every finger at every fret in an alternating two up-two down pattern. Her accuracy and dexterity were remarkable, but the true ring of every note was amazing.

I was captivated.

She stopped at the fifth fret, and the notes bounced around the room until their energy was spent. She looked up and raised her eyebrows with a grin on her face. I nodded, a huge smile on mine. A bond formed, and I saw who she was and who she could be.

"I'm going to kill him."

Her grin vanished.

"I need to break into the house and find all the videos. Then, I'm going to kill him."

She placed the guitar on the stand and walked quickly down the hall into the spare room, coming out with the backpack in her hand. I didn't want her to go, but I wouldn't stop her from leaving if that's what she wanted.

After putting the pack on the end of the coffee table and reaching inside, she came out with something in her hand, looked at me, set it down, and nodded.

~~

John had scheduled his vacation in order to spend some quality time with his daughter during her Christmas break. He'd been waiting for a long while.

When bound to the bed, Mary pretended not to like it, but he knew better. She'd only struggled to entice him. As time passed though, he worried she might act differently once the restraints were removed and began to realize he'd have to do something – something permanent.

But then Mary gave in to her desire. She became eager for his attention, and her moan was . . . deeper. Hearing it without the gag had shaken him to his very core.

He didn't want to kill her now – now that she wanted him, too. He was sure of it. Mostly.

When he left for work yesterday, he'd sent the texts from the garage as insurance to keep her quiet, a reminder that he owned her. No one would believe she'd been forced into anything, not after seeing the videos.

It hadn't occurred to him she might leave. He tried to reach her, but she wouldn't answer her phone. He left messages expressing his concern she'd 'run away again,' pleading with her to stay away from 'those boys and their drugs,' and to 'please call' so he could come for her. Those messages would provide the school, or the police, a reasonable explanation for her sudden disappearance.

He hoped she came back soon and thought she would, convinced he'd awakened a hunger inside her. If she didn't, he'd at least have her on video, which reminded him to get the memory stick from the truck.

Right after he got off work tonight.

~~

I'd left the house this morning after she put the key on the table, having things to do, places to go, and people to kill. The time seemed to fly by as I went about my day with purpose, and, as I drove home, I thought about my night and what lay ahead. It needed to be done.

And I needed to do it.

Earlier, I'd walked the forest searching for an optimal location before putting shovel to ground. Remoteness was an important factor but not the only consideration.

A makeshift grave covered with leaves and branches could be exposed when the rain fell, and the wind blew. Over time, weeds and undergrowth might hide it naturally, but a conspicuous bare spot would be visible until then.

I found an acceptable spot in a thicket of course grass surrounded by bush-like foliage several yards to the east of a very small creek. After cutting the grass like sod, I rolled it back and between the thicket, dug my hole, and tossed the shovel inside as a crescent moon rose through the trees.

Now, I was dirty, sweaty, and tired. I didn't sleep much last night and wondered if she'd gotten any herself. Just in case she was catching up, I slipped quietly into the house.

She was gone, and a deep sense of loss swept over me.

When the back door opened, her smile turned around when she saw me. She must have seen my distress, and the look in her eyes both gladdened and broke my heart.

"I need a shower."

"Yup."

The hot water soothed the sadness I'd just experienced. Not one to ride emotional roller coasters, I'd been to the top, bottom, and was already heading for the first hairpin turn. I shook my head and chuckled.

In less than twenty-four hours that little girl had moved into my heart, and my life was not my own anymore. And, on top of that, she played a better guitar than I did!

The little shit.

I dried off and dressed for success, donning slick, dark, comfortable, DNA intolerant attire. I was ready and stepped into and down the hallway.

It's showtime, folks.

Tennis shoes were on her feet, and a jacket sat nearby.

"No."

"I'm going," she said, looking resolute.

She was serious.

I went to the kitchen and made a turkey and roast beef sandwich with Mayo on both pieces of bread, a slice of swiss cheese, lettuce and tomato on top. A little salt and, *Voila.*

"Have you eaten?"

"Yup."

"Want something to drink?"

"Nope."

Placing the snack on a plate, I took an orange Crush with me to the living room. When I tried to set the soda down, I got a look. I put the can on the plate, a coaster on the coffee table, the soda on the coaster, a placemat by the can, the plate on the mat, and my behind in the big chair.

I looked at her looking at me and rocked and ate my sandwich. Her irises were a cobalt blue that pierced and penetrated, and I wondered if mine had any such qualities.

She didn't need to be part of this. She'd been through a lot. Then again, she'd been through a lot. Maybe she needed to be part of this?

As long as I couldn't stop her, I thought of how to include her that wouldn't alter the plan or significantly raise the level of risk. I swallowed the last bite of sandwich and washed it down with just enough orange left in the can to be refreshingly satisfying.

"Can you drive?"

"A little."

"How little?"

"I can push on the gas, push on the brake, and turn the wheel thingy."

Smartass. She was definitely making my like-o-meter needle dance. She was also turning into a chatter box.

"Just one more thing before we go," I said.

She raised an eyebrow.

"That fret run this morning, the really fast one?"

She looked puzzled and nodded.

"You missed a note."

She grinned and shook her head.

"All right, then. Let's go get your father."

"Yup."

~~

After a heavy and fitful sleep, Watson yawned and stretched, the pain from the shock collar still resonating through his mind and body. He looked at the moon and realized he'd slept all day and most of the night.

What the heck?

He sniffed around the tree again, getting agitated because of the still strong stench of hopelessness left by Mary the night before. He walked back up the lane to the paved road and stopped a few miles further down at the intersection. Confronted with multiple scents of her, he went with that old Retriever adage, '*When in doubt, strongest in the snout.*'

Watson turned left and hurried with his nose in the air, his eyes on the bright dog star in the sky.

chapter seven

The night was a beautiful blend of bright stars, dim moon, and cool breeze. She took long, easy strides, forcing me to quicken my step. When I asked her to amble, she said she was.

I'd driven in and around the neighborhood earlier this morning, searching for security cameras while looking for garage sales, and saw a faint trail with overgrown grass and overhanging leaf-laden branches about three miles from her house. I had her drive there to assess her proficiency. Turned out, it was another thing she was good at.

The backpack contained items from my basic starter kit: duct tape, zip-ties, gloves, hammer, knife, and the gun. But with any luck, I wouldn't have to shoot him.

I asked if there was a way we could reach her back yard without activating any neighbor's motion-detecting lights.

"Yup."

When we came to the edge of the trees, I put on some latex gloves. It was dark except for a light inside the house.

"What room is lit?"

"Kitchen."

I told her to stay put and crossed the backyard to the garage window to peek inside. His truck, and presumably his person, was gone. I turned and nodded.

She came over and held out her hand. I gave her the key, and she walked to the door and opened it. I followed her inside and closed it behind me. She started to move, but I reached out and touched her arm, a finger to my lips. We stood for a moment and listened.

"Alright."

I walked past the kitchen and its light to the dark living room, sat on the couch and reached into the backpack. She followed and sat next to me, looking briefly down the hall. I checked my watch and saw it was midnight-thirty. Unless he had other plans, he'd be home from work soon.

She got up suddenly and walked to a closed door in the hallway. Before opening it, she turned and looked at me.

"Don't come in here."

I didn't understand, but it was her business.

"If you're still in there when he comes into the house, don't make a noise and don't come out. Okay?"

She nodded.

"Where's his bedroom?"

She turned the knob and pointed down the hall. When the door opened, I saw a flower against a white background on the headboard of her bed.

~~

He punched out a half-hour early and walked quickly across the parking lot to his truck., unlocked the door, pulled the handle, climbed in, closed the door, and locked it. He glanced around furtively, retrieved the phone from his pocket, and found the video he'd been thinking about all night, the one whipping him into a frenzy.

His finger shook as he tapped play.

Mary was lying on the bed, her breasts heaving, her fingers probing, and her eyes begging him to touch her.

She wants it too much to walk away, he thought. Mary was probably at home right now, waiting for him. What did she say yesterday before he left?

Wake me when you get home.

He put the truck in reverse, backed up, and shifted into drive before the gears could catch up, making a grinding noise. He didn't notice he'd run a stop sign a block away.

The damned garage door tortured him by its slowness to open. It had been hard since the video and he hoped she was home so he could bury himself inside of her.

After closing and locking the door, he took off his shoes, walked to the kitchen, and saw her jacket on the counter.

She's here!

He turned off the kitchen light and crept into her room, wanting to take her by surprise. His hunger was stronger than ever and he lifted the blanket, ready to devour her.

But the bed was empty.

When the toilet flushed, he smiled and moved to the door, eager to give her what she wanted, what she'd come back for. He stuck his head into the hallway after the loose board creaked. A gun pressed into the soft muscle under his chin, and a pair of hard eyes glared at him.

"If you move or make a single sound, I'll kill you where you stand."

Wet warmth flowed down his leg.

"The rest of your life begins now and lasts only as long as you do what I tell you, without hesitation or comment. You won't be given another chance. Do you understand?"

He wanted to say, *yes, hell yes, whatever you want,* but was told not to move or make a sound. He began to panic, convinced he was looking into the eyes of certain death.

"Blink twice for yes, once for no."

He blinked twice so fast; he worried it would be mistaken for once. But he didn't dare try to blink again.

"When I tell you to move, do it slowly. Every time. Do you understand?"

He blinked twice. Slowly.

"Come into the hall."

He moved into the hall.

'Turn to your left."

He turned to his left. The gun pressed hard under his right ear in the notch between the jaw and skull as a hand grabbed his shirt from behind

"Stretch out your arms on each side and put your hands on the wall."

Yes, he thought.

"Get on your knees."

Yes, yes!

The collar pulled against the front of his neck as the grip tightened. He coughed when his knees hit the floor.

"You're going to feel some pressure on your throat but go with it. Now, lean forward and lay on your stomach."

He blinked and started to choke but kept moving until his forehead felt the coolness of the hardwood floor.

"This is when you decide whether you die here or make it out of the house alive, I really don't care which. I'm going to zip-tie your hands behind your back. If you fight, we're done here. If you comply, I won't tighten them so much your hands fall off from lack of circulation. Do you understand? Let's pretend I can see your eyes."

He blinked twice – no more, no less. His hands were bound in five seconds, his feet in three.

"Just for shits and giggles, kiss the floor. You don't have to make-out with it. I mean, you don't have to use tongue – although that might be fun. Just smooch it for now."

After being stepped on and walked over, he lifted his head to see a backpack being pulled from behind the planter in the living room.

"I imagine you'll try to look around while my back is turned, and I'd give you a little credit for being ballsy if you did. But if I see it, I'll take it as disobeying, and, if you do that, I'll just wrap this up and call it a night."

He puckered and pressed his lips against the wood, moving his eyes up when the man returned and kneeled. A black shoe was all he saw until his head was pulled back.

"Now, first things first. Did you take a peek at me? Be honest now."

The words were light, even friendly, but those eyes were not. They were deadly. He blinked once, and then once more as the tears began to form. They could be caused by the strain building in the burning muscles of his neck, but he knew better. He was scared to death.

"Good. I appreciate your being honest. I wish more people were. Now, instead of killing you, would you like to earn more time to live? Maybe answer a few questions?"

He watched the knife spin around like a top, the sharp end making a small hole in the floor while the fingers twirled the handle. He blinked twice – twice.

"I'm relying on your complete honesty here, because I have solutions for any problems you try to give me. If you tell the truth, you'll live longer. In fact, you'll be riding down the road in a few minutes. Sound good?"

Two blinks, two blinks.

"Tell me how many videos you made, where they are, and cameras, laptops, tablets, phones . . . get the picture? Assume I've already looked around and found a few things. If you lie, I'll know. If I even think you're lying, I'll burn the house down with you alive in it. And if you hesitate for one second to answer me, I'll use this knife and take your eyes. Now, do you understand?"

Oh God, Oh God, he thought over and over. It was the first time he'd asked himself why this was all happening. He'd been too frightened to form the question, and it now dawned on him that he could die. Soon. He needed time. He had to earn more time.

He glanced up and saw the knife go into the backpack before doing what he'd been told – make-out with the floor, tongue and all, as if his life depended on it.

Because it did.

The one small part of his brain not totally engaged in trying to save his life thought the backpack looked familiar. He heard the creak of the floorboard behind him but didn't dare stop and lift his head, even when she spoke.

"Ready?"

I nodded and asked if she'd seen enough.

"Yup." She'd watched it all from the bathroom at the end of the hall.

I knelt and pressed the gun barrel inside his left ear. "You can stop kissing now but keep your head down. When I tell you to lift it, do it slowly and as high as you can. She's going to put a rag over your nose, and you're going to take five deep breaths. Not shallow ones, but full, lung filling inhalations. How many are you going to take? Speak."

"F-f-five."

"Good. You'll keep your mouth closed and your head up. If you fail to comply, you die. If you try to move, or resist, or bite her, you die – not the quick death a bullet would bring, but the slow, agonizing one from that fire I spoke of earlier. Understand?"

He blinked and blinked and blinked. His eyes were still blinking when told to raise his head, and he didn't stop inhaling until he didn't know he wasn't.

"Get some garbage bags. Pack what you need and then what you want, but don't make a mess. Try to make it look like nothing is missing. And no more than three bags, okay?"

She nodded.

"I'm going to find the things I missed, then wrap him in a blanket and clean the hallway." I glanced at my watch. Only twenty-three minutes since I'd put the gun to his chin.

"We leave in ten minutes. I'll put him in the cargo seat, and we'll throw the bags on top of him."

She nodded and frowned. Maybe she didn't want her stuff sitting on her soon-to-be-dead Dad?

"Is there room for my guitar?"

Uh, hell yeah.

"Yes."

Her eyes twinkled, and it seemed perfectly normal to smile at each other as her father lay unconscious at our feet.

After wiping down the hallway, I dragged the blanketed body to a door that opened to the garage. His wallet, keys, and phone sat in the console of his truck; the laptops, tablet, cameras, and other items double-bagged and ready.

The flash-drives were in my pocket.

She left two bags, the backpack, and a guitar case by the side door and then walked away. I duct taped the blanket around his body and was about to cover his mouth when she returned and handed me an oversized ball-gag.

"Put this on him first."

I could only imagine the extent of what happened to her and wasn't sure I wanted to *know*. After the truck was packed, I dug into the backpack for some fresh latex gloves and put the old ones in the throwaway bag.

"Do I need to wear any?"

"Not yet. Your fingerprints are all over the truck, right?"

"Yup."

"You'll have to wear some again when you drive home. And keep them on while you unload the van. Stay in the house and wait till I get back. I shouldn't be more than a day. Don't answer the door, don't go outside, keep the lights off at night, and be cognizant of your surroundings. Do you know what cognizant means?"

"Do you?"

We grinned and shared the moment.

"I want to be there when he goes in. I want to see it."

She was serious. Again.

"Listen, I understand. I do. But the chances of getting caught, and having to explain why we did this, increases significantly if you're there. We'd have to alter the plan we're in the middle of, and that's not smart."

She considered my words. At least, I thought so as her eyes never left mine.

"Look, I'm not going to make a video and show you later because, well, you know why. But if you really want to know about it, I'll tell you. All of it. Every detail, if you like. The truth and nothing but. I'll always tell the truth if you ask for it. I hope you'll do the same with me."

Her expression softened, and she nodded.

"One last thing. Don't throw away any of his stuff. We need to look at everything, emails, videos . . ."

Her face fell immediately. When the tears threatened, she put her head down and started to cry. Maybe the trauma of her ordeal had resurfaced. I wouldn't want to relive that abuse by seeing those videos, either.

"I'm sorry. I'll do it. I need to know if he shared them with anyone. I don't want anyone to see you like that."

Her eyes raised and gave a look that pierced my heart.

"I don't want *you* to see me like that. I did things. I had to *do* things. To get away . . ." She started to sob.

I didn't know how to comfort her and didn't presume she'd want me to hold or even touch her. She probably wouldn't want anyone to touch her for a long time.

"Nothing is going to change what I think about you. You're a strong young lady, and that strength helped you

lar e hale

overcome an evil betrayal of trust. Whatever you did, had
to be done. I believe that. And I'll kill anyone who tries to
hurt you by saying otherwise."

She stepped forward and hugged me, her head pressed
hard against my chest. I held on and stroked her hair until
the storm of emotion became a light drizzle. When she
leaned back and looked up at me, her eyes said it all. They
said everything. I wiped the tears from her cheeks.

"Ready?"

"Yup."

~~

He stood and looked in the driver side window.

Huh. I didn't know she could drive.

Watson came across the scent at the intersection of
trail and road but wanted to examine the hidden van before
following her. She wasn't alone, and she wasn't in distress.
That surprised him. What had turned her despair into calm
determination in such a short space of time?

Not that he put anything past her. Mary was bright and
capable, even by Retriever standards, and he'd sometimes
marvel at her innate abilities and talents. He walked back
to the road and took a smell around.

Why would she go back to her house when so many
terrible things had happened there?

He trailed her, careful to duck out of sight whenever a
vehicle approached. Yvette had probably already filed a
missing Retriever report, and he needed to see and talk to
Mary before being apprehended.

You'll never take me alive, copper.

He'd heard an actor say that in a film they'd watched on
movie night. He loved her, but Yvette's affinity for old, old
movies had become a sore spot with him. No matter how
many times he told her what he wanted to watch when
asked, she always put in 'an oldie, but a goodie.'

I know she knows I know what she's doing, he thought.
But she doesn't know I know she better knock it off.

Watson wasn't sure the collar would shock him when
he reached the perimeter of the neighborhood but expected

it probably would. He stuck his nose over first when the boundary was reached, and then his head.

Yowza!

He could try to tough it out and suffer the pain, and would, if Mary was in distress, but he wouldn't be in any condition to help her if the need arose. Better to get rid of the damned thing. If he could cut the collar, made of a heavy cloth-like material with wiring embedded inside, he might at least short circuit the connection.

He walked by the tree line to look for something sharp. Fortunately for him, but a sad commentary on the human condition, there were many beer bottles strewn about

Why beer, by the way? He didn't get it, preferring a nice, flavored toilet water to the bland taste of hops.

Different nogs for different dogs, I guess.

Finding a suitable bottle, he picked it up by the throat with his mouth, closed his eyes, and broke it against a tree, leaving a nice jagged edge. He secured the neck of the bottle with his front paws and began the slow and careful process of cutting the collar instead of himself.

It took time, a long time, before it began to loosen its stranglehold on his neck. When a pair of headlights came into view, he hid behind a tree until they drove by. He resumed his battle with the bottle but stopped when something in the air caught his nose.

Is that ... Mary!

Watson cut himself repeatedly in his hurry to be rid of the collar. It didn't cross his mind he could safely run after her as she was now beyond the electronic boundary.

He wouldn't realize it until she was long gone.

~~

Petersen was heading home after a particularly long afternoon-into-late night shift. It wasn't the time away from the station that added to his day; in fact, being out on the street was the best part of it.

It was the paperwork, or more accurately, the typing of information into his computer. The unrelenting inputting was required for everything from bank robbery to branches hanging over a neighbor's property line.

It's because of the times we live in, he thought.

In an effort to be more transparent, but mostly to cover the department's liability, all incidents involving the police were now documented and entered into the daily report. Even when the incident was already recorded on the new body cameras worn by patrolmen.

A pair of headlights made him squint, and the driver appeared to nod as the truck went by. Petersen couldn't tell if it was driven by a man or woman, but it was appreciated. He didn't receive a lot of regard from the citizenry.

About a mile and a half in front of him, another vehicle pulled out of the trees and turned right.

Petersen spun a tale about a romantic, but illicit, tryst, and how the two drivers had gone to such lengths to cover their tracks only to be discovered by an unknown variable – himself. He smiled and remembered that age old saying, *'Man makes plans and God just laughs.'*

Only a few miles from home, he decided to put a face to the lady in his tale of ill-fated lovers by speeding up. Then again,, and considering the times he lived in, it might not be a woman driving the van ahead and the man, the truck. Could be the other way around.

Or maybe even a rendezvous between two women?

He grinned and let loose his imagination for a few seconds until a grimace marred his face when the picture in his mind changed. Could be two men . . .

Not that it mattered to him what two consenting males did, but he preferred the form and function of the female. Especially the one at the house.

Petersen saw the driver in the van by the glow of its dashboard light as he drew alongside. A young woman looked over, nodded, and stuck up her hand in a wave. He waved back and drove by, grinning to himself.

Two nods from two citizens was a good end to his long day. He turned left, careful not to hit the dog running across the road, and thought about the warm dinner and the warmer wife waiting for him at home.

chapter eight

After turning onto the forest road with its dirt lanes, I glanced in the rearview mirror, seeing nothing but dark. Two miles down, I heard movement behind me. He was coming around at just the right time, and I thought about that symmetry, the pause-giving kind.

Maybe there *was* a God?

I checked the rearview again, shut off the lights and turned down the lane – the lane of pain. It sounded like a blues song. Maybe I'd write one to commemorate the occasion. A hundred feet in, I stopped and got out of the truck, taking the roll of duct tape with me. I quickly put a double layer over the taillights.

The moon was bright enough to see the reflection on a piece of foil I'd nailed to the tree earlier in the day. I drove past it and turned around where the trees weren't as close to the lane before returning to the foil. He started to cry when the truck shut off, and I tried to put him at ease.

"Quiet, now, and listen. I brought some shoes for you, and I'm thinking you might like to take a walk and stretch your legs. You could breathe in the cool air, smell the forest, and feel the ground beneath your feet. It will give you some time to calm yourself and prepare."

His sobs were getting louder.

"It's alright to cry. I understand. Just do it quietly."

I turned and looked him stone-cold in the eyes.

"Cause if I have to say be quiet one more time, I'll stick that knife in your eye to remind you."

I could see the difficulty he had in getting himself under some measure of control and gave him three seconds. He blinked twice.

I turned back around and gazed out the windshield, marveling at the magnificence of the universe.

"Here's what I'm offering. If you take a peaceful stroll with me, I won't hurt you when we get to the end. Which is better than you deserve. You took something that didn't belong to you and had your fun. Now, I want you to walk into that grave and take your punishment."

I positioned the rearview mirror so I could see him. So he could see me.

"If you make a fuss, I'll treat you to five minutes of pain that'll feel like hours and throw you into that hole anyway. Do you understand?"

Two blinks, two blinks, two blinks.

He walked quietly through the forest, except for the weeping, and didn't offer any resistance until I lowered him inside and told him to lie on his back. He started to sob and tried to scream but stopped when I reached for the knife.

I was careful to keep the soil from his face, throwing it in without hurry. When the earth grew heavy on his chest, and his breathing became labored, I held the shovel over his eyes and watched them widen as the dirt came for him.

~~

Watson sat for a minute to catch his breath after walking down the long driveway. He'd followed her scent for miles after she passed him in the truck. The stupidity he felt for not recognizing where he'd been in relation to the boundary was softened by an understanding of his state of mind at the time – and his success in finding her through smell and dogged determination.

The house was dark and quiet when he called to her. After the door opened, she fell to her knees, hugging and kissing and rubbing and scratching him.

~~

At a rundown gas station with bad lighting, I used his credit card to buy gas, careful not to leave fingerprints but wanting to leave a clue. A mile from the station, I pulled over and turned off the lights but not the truck before powering up his phone.

Mary. Her name was Mary. She seemed like a Mary.

I didn't find anything in his emails indicating he'd been sharing information, or any pictures or videos attached to any text messages. It looked like he'd kept her to himself. There *were* pictures and videos in his Gallery, some with her engaged and others with her helpless and tied to a bed. I recognized the gag she'd handed me and regretted not making him suffer instead of letting him off so easy.

I transferred everything to the SD memory card and put it in my pocket with the flash-drives. I searched his wallet and left the contents alone, except for a photo of her. She looked about twelve with a smile that melted your heart. I saw the promise of who she would be someday and hoped it could still be kept.

The picture went inside my pocket, and I stepped out of the truck and smashed the phone on the road, throwing it, and the wallet, into the ditch alongside the highway.

After another two-hundred-eighteen miles, a truck-stop loomed on my left and a stretch of undeveloped land lay ahead. Some trees sprung up a few miles further on, and I parked behind them as sunrise began to break.

I got out of the truck and stretched out the kinks before closing the door with my elbow, leaving the keys inside with hope that someone would move it on down the road.

After removing the latex gloves, I stuffed them in my pocket to toss along the way before catching a ride home. I waited for an empty highway and jogged to the other side with the pack on my back, wondering if she'd stay a while.

And how it would feel if she left.

chapter nine minutes ago

"I mean it, Dax. I'm not going to let them take me away," Mary said, the intensity in her voice driving home the point. She wasn't going anywhere, come hell or high.

"Well, I don't want you to go. You or your little dog."

The clicking on the hallway floor grew louder as Watson walked up and took his place by her side. I liked to get a rise out of him. He was bright and articulate, according to Mary, with telepathic abilities and a good sense of humor. I didn't know about all that, but I trusted he'd protect her.

"It's probably just what Detective Williams said. They're running down vans. But we should proceed as if it's something more and be careful just in case. You'll have to be diligent and keep a low profile, especially when I leave for the weekend. And you . . . will have to keep the barking to an absolute minimum."

Watson cocked his head and said, *I don't bark, I speak.* At least that's what I construed. He was a great addition to this do-it-yourself family, and I leaned back in the big chair.

I'd heard the love you feel for your children was unlike any you'd ever know, and now I understood its meaning. The thought of losing her caused an unfamiliar flicker of fear to cross my mind. I couldn't let that happen.

I really couldn't.

"Maybe you should postpone your trip?"

I nodded. It would be the comforting thing to do, the one most likely to ease my concern. Other than playing at Scallop Cove and a few out of town gigs, I hadn't gone out much since ditching the truck on the highway months ago.

"I know. That might be a way to go. But, assuming I'm being watched, I don't want to alter any plans they might be aware of. Like playing the gig I've been hired to do, information they could easily get by asking around the Cove. You know how I feel about suspicion, it leads to observation, which leads . . ."

". . . to scrutiny and complication. Yeah, I've heard you mention it a few hundred times," she said with a grin.

I called her grin and raised her a smile.

"Besides, I need to stop by the cabin, our possible home away from home, or in this case, somewhere else to be. If the detectives are just doing a routine check, we could be gone in two weeks. Three tops."

Watson liked the sound of that. He'd be happy wherever Mary lived, but he agreed. They needed to leave St. Vincent before the police got suspicious and made trouble for them. He felt bad for Yvette, and hoped he'd find a way to let her know he was alright. But his place was with Mary. And hers with him.

"I heard you practicing *Little Wing* before the police showed up. You planning on trying it out tonight? I could show you how to play it," she said with a twinkle in her eye that grew by the second. "Correctly."

~~

Every time I drive by, I ask myself the same question. *Can I live with it?*

Yes. I most certainly can.

Since putting him in the ground, I check my emotional dipstick regularly, and I'm good. It's not that I don't care about what I do – I do. I wish there was another way to rectify the problem of people treating each other badly, but I don't see one on the horizon.

I thought about my upcoming trip to Destin on the way to Scallop Cove. The real reason I'd taken the gig was to investigate, and possibly eliminate, a man who repeatedly beat his ex-wife. The mother of his child.

I'd heard the story on the local news. She'd divorced him three years ago and had been granted two restraining orders but was in the hospital all the same. The police hadn't arrested him because they couldn't prove he did it, because she couldn't identify who'd attacked her.

Bullshit.

That woman was scared to death, and that man would kill her eventually if nothing was done to prevent it. I could prevent it. I could prevent the hell out of it.

It was risky, though. More so than the others. The woman lived in the same town I'd be playing in, and the chances of my finding the truth *and* the ex-husband in such a short time were slim. Still, it was worth the hundred and eighty-four round-trip miles to try.

I didn't like leaving Mary, but I couldn't turn a blind eye to that woman's suffering.

Hopefully, he hadn't laid a hand on his kid.

That'll piss me off.

The crowd at the Cove was jumping and I had fun, playing loose and only making one or two mistakes every other song. I decided to finish the show with *Little Wing*. Before attempting any difficult song, I liked to wait until the people were happy, talky and a little drunk. My mistakes then become less noticeable and more tolerable.

I started off beautifully, as always, and made the strings sing with that burning tone I loved to hear. My vibrato was spot on, and I played the simple solos with ease, moving my head in a *blues* way – up and down, side to side, scrunched-up face when I bent a particular note.

You know, looking cool.

My eyes were wide open as I neared the difficult part of the second section, the one I'd been practicing when the police knocked on my door this morning. I moved into it like I owned it, hitting every note at every fret and bending every string to my will. I was killing it

Of course, since I'd taken the time to pat myself on the back, I had to improvise to cover-up a couple of mistakes. I smiled knowing Mary would have rolled her eyes – not because I blew it, but because of *how* I blew it. She'd shake her head and say I lacked discipline.

I received a smattering round of applause afterward and used my best Elvis impersonation to show appreciation. "Thank you. Thank you very much."

Everyone gave a good-natured laugh.

"Thanks for coming out tonight, folks. Drive home safely, and don't forget to tip your waiter, uh, waitress, uh, waitperson. What the hell, your guitar player, too."

I got another laugh and a bit of a surprise. Detective Williams was clapping, smiling, and looking at me with those eyes. I gave her a nod and packed up my equipment: drum machine, loop machine, microphones and stands, guitars, amps, cords, speakers, and various foot pedals for various sounds. When finished, I turned around and there she was, holding a drink in both hands.

"I asked for a beer, but the bartender said you'd rather not. Instead, he gave me your favorite. A Fog Cutter? Heavy on the papaya juice, light on the grenadine, somewhere in between with Bacardi rum. Right?"

Her eyes smiled at me, making it difficult to keep from being drawn to her. Why was she here? Coincidence?

"What, no umbrella?" I asked, bringing the smile to her lips. After accepting her gift, I walked us to an empty table.

You planned for many eventualities in the preparation for any project and being questioned by the police was certainly one of them. But her likability was a contingency I hadn't taken into account.

"Detective Williams, thanks for the drink. It's nice to see you again. And so soon."

"Natasha. You can call me Tasha, Mr. Palmer."

"Dax, please."

"Dax. I like your name. How did you come by it?"

"My dad was a huge Star Trek fan. Watched every episode of every series, from the original to the last spinoff, including all the movies. My namesake is from a character on the Deep Space Nine space station."

"So, you're a Trill symbiont. Fascinating. Are you the dominant personality, or do you share one with your host?"

I grinned and regarded her with new interest. She had potential. I raised a brow with the question in my eye.

"I'm told my mother was a Trekkie way before we called ourselves Trekkers. And I've also seen everything Star Trek," she said.

"What's your middle name, Tasha?"

58

She broke into a full smile without the slightest hint of embarrassment. "Yar."

We shared a moment of connection. I could like her. And she could take my new family from me.

"So, did you find more vans fitting the description since I saw you twelve hours ago?"

Damn it!

I'd just made a mistake. Her expression hadn't changed, but her eyes lit up. The ones I'd noticed this morning. The same ones I thought could be trouble.

Tasha, her curiosity tweaked, considered his question. She hadn't said that on the porch, and normally someone wouldn't turn *trying to account for all of them* into *fitting the description*. Which, of course, was exactly what she'd been doing - trying to find a van fitting a description given by a tired patrol officer driving home after a very long day.

"We found three," she said. "We're heading west tomorrow. Should locate another five or six if we're lucky."

A natural progression in the budding conversation would be to ask her the reason for finding the vehicles, but there was risk in doing so. My brain commenced working on that conundrum and promised to get back to me.

"Do you remember the Stewart family disappearance? Happened around five months ago," she asked.

Yeah, I remember.

"Father and daughter left town around Christmas?"

"Yes. They drove into the night, and no one's heard from them since."

I nodded and said nothing.

"Well, the father's truck was found three hundred miles away. We recovered some prints, and they led us to a couple of low-level, low-life brothers running a meth lab in their trailer. They said they found the vehicle, took it home, and then gave it to a friend who drove it to visit his family. He ran out of gas on the way, pushed it into an overgrown culvert, and had to hitch hike to his family's farm."

"Hmmm. Find the father and daughter?"

"No. After talking to the low-lifes, I believed their story. Well, as much as you can with meth heads."

I wondered where she was going with this when my brain told me what I already knew – I was damned if I asked, and damned if I didn't.

"And how does this lead to a statewide van search?"

Tasha was careful in the construction of her ruse. The vehicle in his garage, only fourteen miles from the Stewart's home, fit the description Petersen had given. The purpose of this subtle interrogation was to eliminate a possible suspect of a crime she wasn't sure had been committed. If his tree was shaken, she thought, something might fall.

"The night the Stewarts disappeared, a patrolman saw a truck and a van near their neighborhood." She took a long drink from her glass and continued.

"The father's credit card was used at a gas station some eighty miles away a little more than two hours after he'd gotten off work. Maybe it was his truck the patrolman saw, maybe not. If it was, I want to know if the van is connected to their leaving. Thus, the search."

Damn. *The best laid plans of mice and men . . .*

"That's an interesting puzzle you got there, but it sounds like a lot of pieces are missing."

She nodded and prepared to set the trap.

"You're right. The ones I have aren't enough. I need to find those, *missing pieces*, so I can see the complete picture. Until then, I can't know what it are . . ."

A cloud of grief darkened her thoughts, and they sat in silence until it passed. Tasha saw kindness in his eyes and tried to smile but couldn't, knowing the element of surprise she'd hoped would spring her snare was lost.

"I found a piece that could bring clarity to that picture. There was a flash-drive in the glovebox."

No matter how careful you were, you couldn't account for everything, you just couldn't. You built your plan, considered the possible problems, and tried to find suitable solutions. It hadn't occurred to me to search his truck, and now Mary would suffer because of it.

How many people had seen the contents of that drive? How many others would?

I said just enough to give and receive a response.

"And?"

Tasha relied on her intuition. If Dax was involved, he would have shown more interest, more fear, more... what? She didn't know. Just more.

While it would have been satisfying to break the case wide open by way of this casual attempt to see what was what, she was glad he hadn't been part of what happened to that family. *If* anything had happened. Well, something had. She'd seen the videos.

Tasha responded to Dax's raised eyebrow.

"There's evidence on it that could account for their sudden departure in the middle of the night. Something that might explain the why of it all. The van might be relevant. But . . ." She raised her hands slightly, giving a shrug.

I didn't know if I was a real suspect or not but figured I'd find out soon enough.

"Well, I hope it works out for you, Tasha. And them. If they turn up, would you consider letting me know? I'm a little concerned now." And I was. We needed to leave St. Vincent as soon as we could without raising suspicion.

She nodded and looked inside of me for a bit. Of course, I could see her, too.

We finished our drinks, and she offered to help me load the van. Maybe she just wanted to look inside, but I took her up on the offer just the same.

~~

Mary sat at the computer looking over available classes for the fall semester. She was going to take a couple courses in a few weeks as an online student at the University of Montana-Butte under another name.

To keep her mind sharp and active, she'd been trying to complete her high school educational requirements using the internet, mindful of Dax's tenets: suspicion, observation, scrutiny, complication.

She'd added to that canon after the detectives' visit – separation. She was worried about being taken from Dax. And Watson.

They'd discussed a variety of things that could happen, but Mary was adamant that any contingency plan adhered to a singular solution – keeping the three of them safe, happy, and, above all, together.

They'd agreed she should stay in the house during the daytime and only go outside for extended periods at night. She should keep up with her studies, her playing, and especially, her spaghetti making. Dax liked her sauce.

She also needed to prepare herself - mind and body - for what *could* happen and make every effort to absolve herself for what *had* happened. The last part was very important to Dax, and that made it important to her, as well. It strengthened her belief she'd done what was right and necessary, making it possible for her to flourish.

They'd discussed what to say to the police in the event they were discovered. She'd tell them her father beat her, forced her to leave with him, and when they'd stopped for gas, she'd run away. After Dax found her, she begged him to keep her hidden, even from the police, for fear of her father. She'd say she trusted Dax and no one else – which was true.

One of her father's videos finding its way to the police worried them most. It would cast suspicion if they were found together. Dax had been adamant about who'd take responsibility if the truth came to light, and she'd agreed at the time but would never let that stand. In fact, she'd do whatever needed doing to keep it from happening.

Watson didn't like the thoughts whirling around in her head. He started to give her the benefit of his opinion but stopped the moment she scratched the sweet spot.

~~

Tasha pulled out of the Scallop Cove parking lot and headed off the cape to the mainland. She hadn't expected much from this *fishing* expedition, but she'd enjoyed the music and the company. Dax was interesting: quick-witted, sense of humor, intelligent, talked little, listened more, and could play a pretty good guitar.

What she hadn't told Dax was that patrolman Petersen also saw a girl driving the van. He couldn't identify her as Mary Stewart but said she didn't look frightened or worried or too young to be driving around at two-ish in the morning.

What she hadn't told Petersen was that the picture she'd shown him of a smiling young schoolgirl wasn't how that girl had looked on her computer at home.

What she hadn't told her partner was that the pretext to go to Dax's house was based solely on what she'd seen. She only mentioned officer Petersen's seeing a young woman driving a van late that night and wanting to check it out. Dom said something about a wild goose chase, and she didn't disagree.

And what she hadn't told Dom or her boss, was that there were videos of Mary and her father on a flash-drive they didn't know she'd found.

When she first saw it in the glovebox, she didn't have an evidence bag with her so it went into her pocket as she continued to search the vehicle. Unfortunately, and maybe due to fatigue, she'd forgotten about it till she got home, which was a chain of evidence violation. She should have jumped in her car and taken it to the station right away but was too tired from the long day.

She put it on the nightstand instead and got ready for bed – shower, shave, blow-dry, brush hair, brush teeth, floss, and lotion applied where needed.

After getting under the covers, she powered up her laptop to read a few paragraphs of W.E.B. Du Bois' *The Souls of Black Folks*. Tasha found his views on vigilantism interesting but unrealistic. The only person she'd trust to hand out that kind of justice was herself.

After struggling to stay awake, she reached over to turn off the light and saw the flash-drive.

What the hell, she thought, already in trouble for breaking protocol. After a cursory scan, she opened a folder named *Babydoll*. There'd been over twenty videos, and she'd been disturbed after watching them.

Tasha yawned as she opened her front door and scratched a niggle at the base of her brain. Although her intuition had cleared the guitar player of suspicion, her logic maintained that Dax's was the only vehicle within a seven-hundred mile radius matching all the parameters of the patrolman's recollection from that night.

But Petersen wasn't sure of two of the plate letters.

She fell asleep thinking about the reason she hadn't turned in the flash-drive as evidence, and why it meant so much to find Mary Stewart.

Tasha knew she'd see him tonight in her dreams.

She always did.

~~

Detective Williams was barking up the right tree, and it made me nervous. I hadn't considered till I saw her tonight, that mine might be the only van she was interested in.

If the patrolman saw it, he probably got the license plate number, or part of it, which would explain the knock on my door this morning. He might have seen who was driving as well, but I thought not. If they knew it was Mary, they would have come with a warrant.

Tasha still had pieces of her puzzle to put together, but I didn't underestimate her in the least. She was intriguing, smart and astute. I gave her high marks for the off-handed way she'd give me information, and then look for a response over the course of casual conversation.

Something had ahold of her, though. Something dark. The pain I saw in her eyes was hard to witness. But I couldn't care about her right now. Right now, I needed to figure out how to keep Mary safe and with me.

Her, and her not so little dog.

~~

Mary heard the soda push the ice around in the glass and the big chair swivel before rocking. She thought about joining him, but Dax wasn't humming. He just rocked back and forth, back and forth.

She'd learned to recognize the squeak of the chair when rocked and knew why it moved slow and steady. Part of the reason had to do with the detectives' visit this morning. She'd spent her day worrying about it, too, and how heartbroken she'd be if the police took her away.

But most of it had to do with his gig, the upcoming performance this weekend.

64

Dax had been traveling around the state the last few months, and his getting offers to play didn't surprise her. Despite protests to the contrary, he was good. Better than they joked about, and he could be even better with a more stringent practice regiment.

But it wasn't the playing component that kept the big chair in motion tonight. It was the killing component.

Mary began to suspect a few weeks ago.

They'd seen a news report about current state laws that did little to protect people from being spied upon, harassed, followed, threatened, killed, and made afraid to live their lives or leave their houses. Restraining orders didn't seem to stop the stalkers from coming to their workplace, confronting them on the street, or breaking into their homes.

All the victims in the report were women – one of them murdered fifty miles away by a man the police suspected but couldn't charge. The case was unsolved, and the investigation stalled due to a lack of evidence.

When the man turned up dead a few miles from a bar Dax had played that night, she mentioned it to him.

"Hmm. Guess his stalking days are over."

It was the satisfaction in his eyes that piqued her curiosity. She could have asked if he was involved but chose instead to ponder and process.

When the next gig approached, she watched him and listened to the late-night rocking, its intensity and length, and compared it to after-gig demeanor and rocking. There was an appreciable difference. Enough to investigate what she thought she already knew.

Suspicion leads to observation, scrutiny, complication. *How easily one flowed to the next,* she thought, better appreciating Dax's maxim.

After a careful internet search, she'd found at least one person killed within ten miles of every bar or club Dax had played. That people were killed while he was in the area wasn't convincing – people died every day. What was compelling was what they were charged with or suspected of: pedophilia, murder, rape, manslaughter. Stalking.

Mary gave considerable thought to what he was doing.

Since her father touched her, she'd undergone a radical transformation about what was right and wrong, just and unjust. Not only as it applied to her, but to every life that had been twisted, torn, or taken. There needed to be punishment, a severe and lasting punishment.

She thought about the strength and support she'd found in this home with this person and knew she wouldn't have survived if he hadn't intervened and eliminated the evil from her life. He had given her peace and security – and she wanted others to have it as well.

So she'd decided to let him do what he needed to do without comment or concern, knowing he would proceed with calm and careful determination. She'd seen it up-close.

Watson lay on the floor next to her bed dreaming, and Mary thought she might join him if he didn't mind. The big chair stopped rocking, and she heard the ice lamenting as Dax emptied the glass and set it down on the coffee table. The springs gave a sigh of relief, and the hall whispered as footsteps moved passed her door.

There better be a coaster under that glass.

chapter ten

A little boy perched on the edge of his chair, and I tapped lightly on the frame of the open door to keep from startling him. He flinched and looked at me then over to the woman lying on the hospital bed. The privacy curtain was drawn, and I could only see her legs.

"Miss Dobson? May I come in?"

The woman didn't answer, and the boy looked back at me with fearful wariness. It's not just what comes out of the mouths of babes that have profound meaning.

"Please, Miss Dobson. I'm here because I care about you. That's all. I don't want you to feel . . . defeated."

She remained silent, and I laid the flowers on the other bed and turned to leave.

"I'm sorry if I've bothered you."

Half-way down the corridor, a small voice called. The boy waved me toward him. As I neared, he stepped back and put some distance between us. Enough to keep from being grabbed, to turn and run if he had to. More than enough to tell me what I needed to know.

Elisabeth Dobson had pulled back the curtain, and the boy positioned himself by his mother as I entered the room.

She looked much older than she was. The jawline was offset, and a bruised and battered face told her story. Her eyes looked older still, but I could see a sliver of strength still alight inside her. She was beaten but not broken.

But she *would* be if things didn't change.

"Thank you for the flowers. That's very thoughtful."

Her voice was strong but tentative. I asked if I could bring a chair near and sit with her for a bit. She nodded, concern and curiosity in her troubled eyes. I pulled up to the bed and looked as deeply as she'd let me. She was hanging on. But just barely.

The boy went back to the chair and picked up his book as his mother and I shared our feelings without saying a word. We sat for minutes that felt much longer, and I reached for her hand and spoke softly.

"I have a friend who had a dog. She loved that dog, even though it never appreciated her. She loved it when it yipped at her, when it nipped at her, and when it barked at her, all the while feeding it and taking care to make the dog feel loved, hoping it would love her back."

I moved my thumb slowly across the back of her hand. "One day, he snapped at her. She didn't know why, or what she'd done to make it happen, but she still loved that dog. The first time he bit her surprised her. Not because she wasn't aware of what the dog could do, she just thought he'd never harm her if she loved him enough. Because love conquers all."

Her eyes filled with tears, but she didn't remove her hand from mine.

"The dog started biting her regularly. So often she'd somehow become accepting of it, as if this was what it was going to be and nothing could ever change it. The first time she went to the hospital, it only took four stitches to close the wound. The next time she almost died, and her arm needed seventeen stitches. And still, somehow, she loved that dog. She came to believe the dog might kill her one day, but she still wouldn't take him to the pound."

Elisabeth was nodding, and her tears began to fall. She held onto my hand as my thumb moved back and forth.

"One day, the dog sniffed at her child. He growled, and my friend knew what had to be done. No matter how he'd treated her, she'd never let him harm her baby. She knew that dog had to be put down. Now and forever."

Elisabeth began to cry, and the boy looked up from his book, ready to protect her. She squeezed my hand and looked at me in desperation.

"Where can I find that dog, Miss Dobson?"

~~

After playing my sets at the Funky Blues Shack, I packed up and drove to Bottoms Up. When he didn't show up after an hour, I tried the other place she'd mentioned.

The Hog's Breath Saloon parking lot was full. I looked for cameras on my way across the lot and saw dark patches of lightlessness where a private word could be had with Mr. Dobson should he be here.

The bartender looked at me with disdain when I sat and asked for a wine cooler, muttering something I couldn't hear but understood. I smiled when he returned, stuck out my pinky finger and took a long pull from the short bottle. I swung the seat around and nearly choked on my drink. There he was, listening to the band, the scar on his cheek more pronounced than the picture on his Facebook page.

Halleluiah.

I swear, I'm going to have to reconsider my thoughts on things that are meant to be. All I had to do now was sit and wait. I'd have a nice chat with him outside and go home to girl and dog. It was all downhill from here.

"Hey. Guitar player."

The singer looked in my direction, and I looked around for a guitar player.

"No man, you. Dax Palmer."

You gotta be kidding me.

"Yeah. Come on up and play something."

So much for destiny. I wouldn't be able to kill him outside the bar now, not with everyone knowing who I was.

"Come on, everybody. Let's encourage Dax to come up and play. I saw this guitar-playin' sum-bitch killing it at Funky's tonight, and I know you're gonna like him, too. Come on, folks," he said, stirring up the crowd.

Mr. Dobson was clapping with the rest of them. Quite a few empty beer bottles stood sentry on his table, and I factored this into a possible, alternative plan should the opportunity arise. If I could leave before he did, maybe . . .

I stepped onstage, took the offered guitar, and jumped into Stevie Ray's, *Testify*, a fast and furious song calculated to get me off the stage ASAP. I was playing the hell out of this beauty of a song and damn if the band wasn't on fire as well. The crowd whooped as we kicked ass and took names. I grinned from ear-to-ear, despite having a killing to attend to, and was a bit overwhelmed by the enthusiastic applause.

I thanked the band and the peoples, but they wouldn't let me off the stage. Dobson ordered another beer, so I played one of my favorites – *The Thrill is Gone*, by the late, great B.B. King. I'd never played it with such soul, and the crowd rewarded me with more robust applause.

Damn, I could get used to this.

Dobson nodded his head and clapped, a hard clap, signifying real enjoyment. I acknowledged his praise with a smile. He smiled back. It was a moment I appreciated.

I told the crowd I'd play one more, *then I got to go*. They objected but stopped when I turned on the Wah-pedal and raked up and down the strings in the syncopated beginning of *Voodoo Child - Slight Return*. The cheering was deafening, and I played the crap out of it, convinced I could've literally patted myself on the back without making a mistake.

I was a guitar-playing God.

The applause started to build as I began the last part of the song using the Wah-Wah. I used every expression in my blues-face toolbox and kept my eyes closed until the end. The people roared, and I felt great. I'd played my heart out, leaving it all on stage, and the band pounded me on the back.

Hell, yeah.

I turned to thank the crowd and noticed one person wasn't clapping, because that one person wasn't sitting at the table in front of me drinking beer after beer. That person, like Elvis, had left the building.

It took fifteen minutes to work through the praise of the crowd, and I wished I could've sat with my girly drink and basked in the glow of their appreciation. The manager asked if I'd be interested in playing some weekend and gave me a business card. I thanked him, removed my hand from his spirited handshake, and walked outside to find Dobson.

He was gone.

His ex-wife didn't know where he lived, and, while I might be able to find an address in a phone book, it would be like pulling a rabbit out of a hat to find the right man at the right place at the right time. I'd run out of viable options.

Wait . . .

Miss Dobson had gone home today. In fact, she'd been released a couple of hours after I'd left her. But he wouldn't go there, not after putting her in the hospital. It would be a totally asinine move only a moron would make.

A Daxism whispered in my ear - *Never underestimate the stupidity of your fellow man.*

I could make a quick run by her house and still find a phonebook if it didn't pan out. I was desperate to eliminate this threat to her life but operating without the benefit of an intelligent plan. Everything was risky, and everything was dangerous. I needed more time.

I considered staying in town for another day as I drove down the street looking for her address. The houses were small, the yards cut and well-kept. Even at two in the morning, it looked like a nice neighborhood, a good place to raise your kids. Dobson was sitting in a car as I drove past her house.

Unbelievable!

It was just blind luck I'd found him and had nothing to do with fate or destiny, right? I parked four-hundred feet to his rear and pondered the possibility of providence. I put on a pair of latex gloves, grabbed what I needed, stepped out of the van, and walked across the street.

He'd parked just outside the glow of the nearest streetlight. It helped keep him hidden and undetected as he watched the house. It helped me, too.

I stepped off the sidewalk and moved behind the car and up to the driver's side window. To his credit, he didn't jump when I knocked. Of course, the sixteen beer bottles left on his table might have contributed to his courage. He looked up at me with a scowl on his face, then turned that frown upside-down. The distinct odor of *MaryJane* wafted when the window rolled down. I rarely smoked the stuff but liked the aroma just fine.

"Guitar player. Whatchu doin' out here? Man, you played *The Thrill is Gone* good. Damn good. Best I heard 'cept for B.B."

He was drunk and high, and his smile induced me to spend a few minutes with him before I turned that upside-down frown back around.

"Thanks, man. I appreciate it. Ain't nobody plays it like the King, though. I could listen to him and Lucille all night."

He nodded and took a drink from the bottle between his legs and a toke from the joint in his hand. He offered me a drag, but I thanked him and said I had a long drive ahead and needed to stay awake.

"Keeping an eye on Elisabeth?"

"Damn straight. That bitch gotta learn what's what and who's who," he said, taking another deep drag and holding it . . . holding it.

"And just what, exactly, does that bitch gotta learn, Mr. Dobson?" He blew the smoke from his lungs, and I took a little into my own. For the road.

"She gotta learn who's boss, who's makin' the rules. And I'll keep beatin' the livin' shit outta her until she . . . Hey. How you know my name?"

"Your teaching days are over, Mr. Dobson."

I plunged the icepick four times in rapid succession. He didn't react at first, and I inspected the pick to ensure the pointy part was still attached. It was, and I slammed it back into his heart and left it there. That made an impression. His eyes got big and bewilderment became fury in a flash.

"What the fuck . . ."

Although I was willing to share his last moments in a quiet, dignified manner, he didn't take kindly to an icepick in his chest and, really, who could blame him?

He reached between the console and seat, and I put a bullet in his eye with the silenced gun in my hand. The .25 caliber slug rattled round his skull, shredding brain tissue and killing him from within.

I thought about leaving the icepick but decided against it. I'd find a place for it along the highway on the way home.

~~

It's the middle of the damn night, for crying out loud.

Thom had to pee. He hated getting old, and he hated having to pee all the time. He saw a flash of light on the way and crossed over to the second story bedroom window. Someone was crossing the street to the sidewalk.

Probably the dome light when the car door opened.

When he found out the next morning a man was killed in front of his house, he remembered the person walking away. When he found out who'd been killed, he didn't remember anything and had nothing to tell the police.

Thank God, he thought. Elisabeth doesn't have to worry about that son of a bitch anymore.

~~

"No, Daddy," she said, as his hand covered her mouth.

"Stop it now, or it'll hurt. It'll hurt, and you'll wish it didn't. Just relax." He pushed himself between her legs, and she could see the pleasure he took in taking her.

Tasha's eyes were wet when she reached to stop the alarm from performing its primary function – rescuing her from her dreams. Her nightmares. She could still smell him, still feel his breath on her neck as he took her over and over, time after time, year after year.

How long? *How long will I keep reliving this?*

Many years ago, she'd gone back to see her father, living alone on the small ranch in the middle of nowhere. He looked the same. The same arrogance, the same crooked smile, the same gleam in his eye.

She'd gone there for an apology, to hear him beg for forgiveness, to plead with her to release him from the torment of his shame. When she saw that gleam, she turned around without saying a word, leaving the farm, leaving Utah, and leaving him.

But he wouldn't leave her. Tasha saw him almost every night, and in excruciating detail.

Before the statute of limitation ran out, she used to think about having him arrested. But as much as he deserved to rot in jail, she couldn't have endured the attention and judgment of her colleagues. Which was silly, because they'd have supported her regardless of what her father said. Even if he'd said she liked it. They wouldn't have believed such a thing, but it would be in their heads. She'd have seen it in their eyes.

And it was true.

Her father had touched her for as long as she could remember, and it had never seemed wrong or unnatural. He was loving, making her feel warm and tingly, and her fervor had only intensified as she got older.

He'd always stressed how private a thing they shared was, and how talking about it with others would be inappropriate and embarrassing. Both for her and for them. *Not everyone is as fortunate to have such a father,* he said, and she'd believed him, feeling sorry for those girls.

When her friends began to talk about sex in their early teens, and what it might feel like, Tasha wondered why their fathers hadn't shown them. Don't they love their daughters? Wasn't it a normal part of growing up?

It only took a few minutes on the library computer for her curiosity to turn into doubt and fear. If she had known then what she knew now, Tasha would have gone to the principal and told her everything. But she was naïve and confused and needed answers from a father she trusted, a man who'd loved her all her life.

He had a gleam in his eyes when she'd asked about it.

"Well, little girl. It's not every father who teaches his daughter the loving ways of the world, and I've been pleased by how much you've learned. You're a natural, sweetheart, something to be proud of. It will lead to good things in life."

"So you're saying this is right? It's legal?"

"Right? Yes. I believe so. Legal? No. Not a whole lot of people feel as I do. Not many would understand. Some might think I've hurt you. Have I hurt you, honey?"

The way he'd asked, so caring and unapologetic, still haunted her. As Tasha sat up on the bed and slipped into her foot cozies, she remembered how she'd answered.

"Well, no. You haven't hurt me."

And when she'd said that, it was true. He'd never hurt or harmed her in any way. There was no physical pain, no emotional pain, no psychological pain, no trauma, no regret, no shame, no death wish, no suicide attempt. All of that would come later.

"I'm glad to hear it. If I'd hurt you, made you feel bad about things, about yourself, well, that would be wrong. Do you feel bad about the things we do?"

"Well, I, uh . . . no. I don't," she'd said, and the older Tasha cringed in the bathroom as she brushed her teeth.

But how could she have answered otherwise? She'd never had a single doubt about what they were doing until that day and couldn't accept what she'd seen on the computer. It would be like eating ice cream all your life then being told it was wrong. Wrong to want it, wrong to eat it, and wrong to like it. It didn't register or make sense.

How could that be? Tasha thought, spitting the toothpaste into the sink with disgust. How can you be abused by your father all those years without feeling it?

Without knowing it?

Intellectually, she understood how. She'd read about it, studied it, and the weight of all that knowledge helped subdue her anxiety. But every morning, she'd wake up in a cold sweat and blame herself for being so naive and stupid.

"Well, we could stop what we're doing," he'd said. "Stop enjoying each other. You enjoy it, right?"

Of course, she had. It made her feel good, grown-up. Special.

"We could stop, or we could not stop. It's up to you, but our business is our business. Saying anything will cause a commotion with people who won't understand. They'll take me away and call you names because they'll be jealous of how good you are at what you've learned."

She stayed another five weeks until the seed of doubt planted in the library came to fruition, forcing her to leave. She'd gone to live with an aunt in Florida and never told anyone anything. Ever.

Tasha washed the tears from her eyes with a warm washcloth, still thinking about the little girl in the dream with her father and the little girl on the video with hers.

Something's gotta give, or something's gonna break. And Tasha knew that something could be her.

~~

Watson loved to run around at night. Without the shock collar, he could go as far and as fast as he wanted. Sometimes with Mary, and sometimes, like now, by himself. He looked at the dog star, Sirius, and the moon.

Must be around four, four-thirty.

Dax should be getting home anytime. In fact, Dax should have been home already, but he wasn't worried. Mary told him some of the things they'd been through, and she trusted and believed in him the way he did her.

She'd been asleep for hours and was having one of her bad dreams. He couldn't share those with her. They were too painful and vivid. He didn't know how she coped, how she managed to put it aside every morning as if her spirit hadn't been broken.

Almost broken. Mary was resilient, and he marveled at her tenacity to move forward and make things better.

That's right, I said tenacity.

People forget Golden Retrievers are one of the most intellectual breeds on the planet, and he could hold his own. Watson was not an animal. He was an intelligent, sentient being taking the world as he found it and trying to make it better with a little humor and civility. He was a renaissance Retriever, a dog's dog, a . . .

He lifted a leg by the bush and let go.

Watson walked through the door Dax installed for him, jumped on the couch, and laid his head on the soft cushion.

To sleep, perchance to dream. He fell asleep thinking he'd make a great Hamlet.

chapter eleven

"Morning, pard. Man, I don't mean to offend, but you look like crapola. Did you get *any* sleep last night?"

Tasha nodded at Dom. "I know, I know."

She didn't say why she hadn't slept well. She never did. "What's going on in St. Vincent proper? Murder, mayhem? Maybe some mischief?"

"There's a new mural on the side of Piggly Wiggly by that art aficionado, Chica Sanguine. It's another masterpiece of spray-can artistry. She makes that doughnut come alive."

He handed her a picture, and Tasha saw what he meant. The doughnut looked real. So did the cop eating it. And the people being robbed behind him while he stuffed his face. She smiled and hoped the artist wouldn't be caught any time soon. Chica was good.

"Oh yeah. Hear about that guy over in Destin? The guy who got picked and popped?" Dom asked.

"No. What happened?"

"He was in his car drinking a little beer, smoking a little weed, you know, relaxing, minding his own business, when *Bam!* – somebody puts an icepick in his heart and a bullet in his brain. A bit of overkill, but he probably had it coming."

"How did he have it coming?"

"He was parked outside his ex-wife's house, violating a restraining order. The police said she'd just gotten out of the hospital he put her in, but they didn't have enough to charge him. Even though he'd been beating her for years . . . Looks like someone said *enough*."

Maybe it was, she thought.

"We got anything doing this morning?"

"We're assisting on an arrest for a parole violation, following up on a smash and grab at Half-Hitch, and we have Court at one. Not too busy, not too slow," he said.

"Alright, let me get some coffee and read the reports."

Tasha poured the russet-colored beverage and took it to her desk. The burning liquid soothed and energized. She picked up the case folder requiring their time in court as a tiny ball in her brain found the hole and fell into place.

"Where did you say that guy got killed?"

"Destin."

She'd gone to Scallop Cove last night to unwind and get a beer, maybe hear some music. Maybe see Dax. When she asked the bartender why the guitar player wasn't there, he said Dax was playing a gig over to Destin. Said there'd been a few gigs lately. She'd been disappointed and didn't know she would be until she was.

Funny, she thought. She liked Dax, and it surprised her because she hadn't liked anyone in a long time.

Funny, she thought again. What were the odds Dax would be using a guitar pick in the same city on the same night the killer used an icepick? She smiled, and then wondered what the odds really were?

"Hey, let's get up and at 'em, partner. We got bad guys to find, and doughnuts to consume," Dom said, looking over at the Piggly Wiggly wall picture.

Tasha shook her head, poured some more coffee, and walked outside to another beautiful day in paradise.

~~

". . . and early this morning, a man was found dead in his car on Peacock Avenue. The man, Jefferson Dobson, had been stabbed and shot outside the home of his ex-wife, Elisabeth Dobson. Miss Dobson was recently released from Sacred Heart Hospital where she'd been recovering from an assault. The police won't comment on the death of Mr. Dobson but did tell our own Rebecca Holloway that a restraining order filed by Miss Dobson against her former husband had been in effect. Mr. Dobson had been arrested numerous times for assaulting his wife but was never charged. He was a suspect in her recent attack, but . . ."

Mary turned the television off and walked into the kitchen to clean up. She bent to kiss the top of Watson's head, giving him the slightest scratch behind his ears and smiling when he glanced at her with *don't tease me* eyes.

He went back to finishing the food in his bowl, and she put the skillet and dishes in some hot, soapy water. As she washed and rinsed, she mulled and pondered.

What Dax is doing is just, she thought, and the benefit to people like Miss Dobson was tangible, something that could strengthen and sustain them.

Mary understood what they felt – both from the abuse and its absence. Knowing they'd never have to face or fear their abuser again was such a liberation it lifted the spirit. It gave a sense that life could be good again, be right again. She knew how important that feeling was and wanted others to experience it for themselves.

She wished there was another way, one that didn't put Dax at risk. But that woman had been beaten over and over, and the police couldn't keep that man from hurting her. It wasn't right, and he had to be stopped.

She thought about the little girl she used to be, the one who wouldn't step on an ant or a crack that might break a mother's back. That little girl wanted everyone to like each other and be kind to one another. She liked to fly, liked to play, liked to learn, and loved her Daddy. But that girl almost died because her Daddy had almost killed her.

And he would have if Dax hadn't found me, she thought and shook her head trying to rid herself of remnants of last night's dream, the one about her evil bastard of a father.

He'd been stopped.

Watson patted her leg with a big, fuzzy paw, and she wondered how long he'd been standing there.

"Hey. Thanks. I was heading to a bad place. Want to go out back for a bit? I'll throw the ball and you can fetch, if it's not unbecoming a dog of your stature."

He looked at her with some worry and some wonder, sure she'd be alright. But there were moments. Maybe he'd talk to Dax about it.

Maybe he'd also ask why it took so long for a human to regenerate? Dax got home around five this morning and wouldn't get out of bed until well after noon.

What's up with that?

~~

There they are.

The redfish he'd been looking for all morning were close to shore. The school was sizeable, two-three hundred fish. His excitement began to build, and he could hardly wait to get a line wet.

Not that he'd keep any. He was strictly catch and release when it came to redfish. The battle was thrilling, and he marveled at their strength and beauty, but he wanted them to live and fight another day. If he wanted fish for dinner, he'd keep a flounder or pompano instead, maybe a speckled trout if it swallowed the hook and was going to bleed out after he'd removed it.

The drone was great for finding schools of redfish and had been a good investment. A lot cheaper than putting a tower on his Dolphin, a flats boat that took the waves well

Steve began to bring it back before getting his *fish on.* As it veered to the right, he spotted a girl and dog playing in the backyard of a house a few hundred feet from the water. If the drone hadn't been so high, he wouldn't have seen them through the trees along the shoreline.

He pushed the control and moved it closer, zoomed the camera and saw the expression on the dog's face as it looked up at the flying contraption. A move to the left and he saw the girl, who raised a hand to block the sun from her eyes.

Oh, yeah, Steve thought. Long legs. Nice rack.

He made the drone wave by tipping the sides. Most of her face was covered, but she smiled and waved back with her other hand. He zoomed in as far as the lens would go. Teenagers didn't look like that when he'd been in school.

Ah, to be young again.

He pushed a button and the drone returned to the boat. After stowing it, he raised the Power-Poles, started the motor, and idled over to the school. He didn't want to spook them and hoped they weren't in too shallow for the boat to get close enough to reach them with his cast.

Steve drifted up and threw the Chartreuse colored jig-head in front of the fish, letting it sink to the sandy bottom. Wham – a red took the bait and ran off, bending the rod tip.

"There he is," he said. It was going to be a good day.

~~

My watch said two-sixteen, and I scratched, stretched, and yawned. I'd just left an interesting dream featuring my telekinetic abilities. Whatever I wanted would come to me, moved and manipulated by my mind.

Attempting to bring this capability into the real world, I concentrated, pulled a Mountain Dew out of the fridge, and brought it down the hall to my room. So far, so good – but I had trouble opening the door.

Maybe my telekinetic reach couldn't exceed my grasp? After setting the soda on the floor, I got out of bed, and put on shirt and shorts.

I hadn't had the recurring nightmare in weeks. Now, all my dreams were fun and adventurous. Righting wrongs seemed to agree with me, and I grinned knowing Miss Dobson's wrong had been righted.

When I opened the door, I half expected to find my morning *Dew* sitting on the floor. The other half laughed at my foolishness as I walked into the living room. Mary was typing on her computer, and Watson was regenerating on the couch, tongue out and snoring.

"Hey, girl."

"Hey, back."

I poured some green, caffeine-rich elixir into an ice-filled glass and read the note on the counter.

~Look in vegetable bin~

A big bowl of cold spaghetti greeted me. The sauce had onion, mushroom, garlic, green pepper, red pepper, sausage, and a lot of hamburger mixed in, all stirred together with fettuccini noodles. A note attached to the parmesan cheese said ~You're welcome~

"Thanks. I appreciate you."

"I know."

Half the container of cheese ended up on the spaghetti, and I took glass and bowl to the big chair.

I watched her with my side-eye periphery, and, without being obvious, she was doing the same. I moved to set the soda on the coffee table and slowly inched it down. She kept typing on her laptop and kept not-not looking at me. As soon as the glass touched the table, the typing stopped.

I looked over with an expression of *what* on my face and saw a *come-on* on her own as she shook her head.

Our eyes were laughing.

"You're like a kid, sometimes," she said, and went back to her typing.

"You, too."

I sat the glass on a coaster but kept the spaghetti bowl. It was mine, all mine, and although Watson was asleep, he'd fight me for it if he knew. I might have shared, but it wasn't a given. After eating most of my breakfast-lunch, I thought about last night and the many mistakes I'd made.

It's a funny thing about mistakes.

If I'd made *any* during the first two songs, I would have begged off stage and left the bar before Dobson did, giving me time to make a better plan than the one I'd implemented.

Now, I was vulnerable. Someone could have looked out a window, or a security camera might have recorded me or the vehicle. I knew of one mistake I'd made for certain - I should have taken a drag of the wacky-weed he offered me. The high I received just from the smoke he'd exhaled made the ride home nice and mellow.

Oh yeah – one more mistake. I shouldn't have pulled into that all-night burger joint with a loopy grin asking for, 'One Giant whopper with cheeeeeese, pleeeese.'

But that kind of fast-food, take out-camera video was usually recorded over after twenty-four hours.

"Hey."

"Yeah?" she said.

I swiveled the chair around, feeling apprehensive and hoping it wouldn't get worse but knowing it would.

"I'd like to talk to you if you're not too busy."

"Sure. Let me save this essay. I have an English paper due on Wednesday." She clicked a few keys, closed her laptop, looked up and raised her eyebrows.

"I stopped by the cabin on the way to Destin and everything looks good. The water works, electricity works, and the roof is still intact. There's a family of raccoons in *your* room, but I think they'll share if you behave."

She rolled her eyes and grinned.

"Something's come up. A detective stopped by Scallop Cove the other night, the same one who came to the house. It was supposed to be a casual coincidence, but it wasn't. I'm not sure if I'm a suspect, but she told me why they were interested in a van like mine. A patrol officer saw one close to your house the night you and your father went missing."

Mary remembered nodding and waving to the officer as if it were a natural thing to do. But she'd been afraid he'd make her stop and tell him about her father.

"He came up beside me. I waved, he nodded, and drove on. But wait . . . why didn't they look for the van sooner if he knew who I was?"

I'd seen the cop, too. Nodded at him, as well, in fact.

"I don't think they thought you could be the driver until they found something in your father's truck, which must have happened recently or they would have looked sooner, like you said."

"What did they find?" she asked with dread.

"A flash-drive in the glovebox. She didn't tell me what was on it, but we should assume the worst."

Mary looked away, alone with her thoughts.

I felt a cold, dank, sticky sweat that oozed inward instead of out as the ticking of the wall clock was amplified by her stillness. I wanted to say something but didn't

When she looked over, the trust in her eyes scared me. If I failed her, it would do irreparable damage. To us both.

"What should we do?" she asked.

"We can go forward with the cabin plan – move out there, keep a low profile, pretend you're my niece, and continue to build a new identity you can take to college and beyond. We've already discussed the pros and cons of living as someone else."

She nodded, and I continued.

"You can go live with your Aunt and Uncle in Michigan, tell them you ran away from your father, and build a life there as yourself."

She glared at me.

"I told you, I am not leaving you. Even if they drag me away, I'll come back. I mean it." And she did.

And she would. I raised my hand and swallowed. She was breaking my heart.

"I know, I'm sorry. Just want to explore every option, do what is best for you."

"Staying together is best for me. Me, and my little dog," she said, looking at a waking Watson.

I swiveled around, asked why he was sleeping the day away, and if he'd like some parmesan with the spaghetti his nose was buried in.

Mary's lips turned up as she watched the exchange. She needed this – the fun and frivolity, the feelings of safety and security she felt with them. This was her family now. She smiled and so did Dax.

"Do you want me to continue?"

She nodded and prepared herself. He had only given her the options of least resistance.

"If the police have videos of you, it changes things. It makes it impossible to keep your life private and increases the probability their existence will be leaked to the press, or worse, the videos themselves. Hopefully, only the detectives working the case will ever see them."

She gazed at the floor and chewed on a strand of hair wrapped around her finger. I knew how it made her feel to be seen like that.

"If we go to the police and tell them how we found each other, it might be better than waiting for them to find us. You could tell them why you were in the woods, why you couldn't tell anyone what happened, and why you wanted to stay with me."

Mary continued to chew her hair.

"The police will assume he went looking for you after you ran away, which his text messages will support. What happened to him will remain a mystery. Unless you want them to know."

She glanced up at me and shook her head. I nodded and told her the worst of it, at least for me.

"They would probably take you into protective custody and question you. I'd petition the court to allow you to stay with me until everything was settled, but they might have you stay with someone else in the meantime. We could be separated for a while. Maybe a long while. But I'd keep fighting for you, fighting for us to be together. It's a risk, but we would be free to be ourselves and live out in the open."

Her eyes pierced me as deeply as they ever had, and, as they began to fill, mine did as well.

"It would be wonderful if I could live with you and Watson without the fear of being taken away. I worry about that a lot. I can't lose you, Dax. I . . . I love you," she said before the tears overflowed and ran down her cheeks.

I couldn't move or speak but felt my own ready to fall. She wiped her eyes with the sleeve of her shirt, and I took a quick swipe at my face when I thought she couldn't see me. She did and started laughing. Me too, and after a couple of minutes, we dried our eyes again.

"Let's see what the next couple of days bring and use the time to reconsider our options. Those we know, and those we haven't thought of yet."

She nodded and opened her laptop, giving me a smile and a twinkle. I rocked in the big chair, appreciating how graceful she was even in the simple act of typing.

"Hey, Mare?"

"Yeah?"

"I love you, too."

"I know."

chapter twelve

The echo of his footsteps welcomed him as he walked through the lobby of the Post Office to the wall of mailboxes. With his key in the lock, he paused to pray.

Why hast thou forsaken me and withheld the generosity of your bounty? Please restore unto me your gifts and let me share in the glory of your revelation.

He slowly opened the thin tiny door, wanting to see but not wanting to look.

It was empty.

"Goddamn it, you selfish piece of sh . . ."

An old lady gave him the stink-eye.

"Sorry, Ma'am. I shouldn't have said that. Have a good day, now." When he walked through the lobby, the echo seemed to mock him, saying, 'Ha-ha, ha-ha, ha-ha.'

Once outside, he took a deep breath.

"Brother-mine, what has become of you? It's been months and not a word, not a text, not a picture, and, for crying out loud, no fucking video."

He mumbled down the sidewalk, shaking his head and trying to compose himself. By the time James reached the car, he was calm and collected. *Daddy, Daddy* greeted him as he sat inside and put the key in the ignition.

"Hi, boys. Were you good for your sister?" He glanced in the rearview at the twins laughing at their sister sitting in the passenger seat.

"Jewels swore, Daddy. She told us to shut the hell up," Joshua said, putting a hand over his mouth and poking his brother, who was doing the same.

"Is that true, Jewels?" he asked his young daughter.

"Daddy, they're monsters. They kept yelling and laughing at each other and wouldn't stop or quiet down. They're exhausting, sometimes."

She frowned at her brothers with affection.

"Is that true, boys? Are you monsters?" he said with a grin, watching them in the mirror.

"Jason might be, Daddy, but not me."

"Nuh-uh. I'm the good one, Daddy," Jason said.

James shook his head and pulled out of the parking lot, thinking about his missing brother.

~~

Every other Wednesday, I ran a kind of amateur night at the Scallop Cove, outfitted with a small drum set and an organ-piano, along with bass, acoustic, and electric guitars. I even brought some tambourines and a triangle or two for those who had the inclination but not the talent.

After setting up, I'd invite people to come up and play – beside me, behind me, in front of me, or instead of me. It was fun, and one of the few times I'd imbibe while working.

I clapped along with the crowd for a young man who'd just rocked and rolled the keyboard playing Boston's song *Smokin'*, which was remarkable given the limitations of the instrument. I took a drink of my drink and asked if anyone else wanted to come up and play.

"I've got one more tune in me if you'd like; otherwise, I'm gonna pour one more drink into me and shut it down. And hey, let's give everyone who's come up here tonight a big round of applause, okay?"

The crowd was generous with their praise, as was I, clapping and giving them my respect. Playing in front of people could be scary. As Kermit the frog said so eloquently, *'it's not so easy being green.'*

A smattering of applause accompanied a lady walking to the front. Her stride denoted confidence, and her eyes sparkled as she stepped onto the stage. When she smiled there was no denying the simple truth – she was beautiful.

"Detective Williams. It's good to see you."

"You too, Dax. Have you forgotten my name, already?"

"Of course not, Lieutenant Yar. So, you play?"

She nodded.

"Which instrument?"

"All of them."

I raised an eyebrow, and she raised her own.

"Impressive."

"It is," she said and picked up the bass, plugged it in, checked the tuning, and tapped one of the microphones.

"Feel like a little Texas Flood?"

Oh, hell yeah.

I played the first three notes, started the drum machine with my foot, and we were off. She sang the lead, and man, could she *sang*. She had a Linda Ronstadt-Melissa Etheridge kind of voice, and as she transitioned from Linda to Melissa, it gave me goosebumps.

We shared the solos – me making the strings scream, her making the bass bellow. I watched her when she didn't know and watched her when she did, and she smiled and watched me back.

After we finished, the people voiced their appreciation, especially for Tasha, and she blushed and got embarrassed from the attention. I encouraged the audience to continue their praise and she looked at me, her eyes laughing and her face getting redder. She was unguarded and childlike and seemed like a kind and decent human being.

Damn it! Now I liked her.

She insisted on helping me get the equipment into the van, and we talked about ourselves in small, genuine ways. Nothing too heavy and nothing too personal. When the last of the items were loaded, I leaned against the van.

"Come on, Tasha. That can't be. I mean, really?"

"It's true. If I'm lying, I'm dying."

Something that could have been merriment lit her eyes, and I didn't know if she was having fun *with* me or *at* me.

"So, you're saying you haven't played bass in five years? Come on."

"Well, sure, I've plunked on one over the years, but I haven't played, not really, and certainly not on stage in front of people. Normally it scares me to death."

"What happened tonight? You didn't seem scared. In fact, you were downright fearless."

"I tried a new drink, your favorite. Fog Cutter, right?"

I nodded.

"The papaya juice was so sweet I couldn't taste the alcohol, so I drank a couple quick ones before it hit me. When I strode to the stage, I wasn't scared because I didn't feel nervous because it was just you, me, and Mr. Bacardi."

She smiled and leaned against the van next to me.

Many thoughts vied for my consideration, not the least of which was her confident use of the word *strode*. You just didn't come across that word outside of literary prose.

Why was she here? To pull on the loose thread and unravel the tapestry of my brand-new family?

With a side-eye, I watched her gaze at the vastness of the night sky, an expression of wonder on her face. There was something engaging about the way she appeared to ponder the universe, with all its grandeur and possibilities. I pondered a possibility of my own.

Maybe I should just tell her? I'd been thinking about it since the night we talked but wasn't sure she'd understand. I might end up making things worse.

"Tasha?"

"Dax?"

"How do you feel about directness?"

"Directness is correctness. Don't you agree?"

I grinned at her wordplay, and her eyes sparkled.

"Remember telling me about the family that left town, and the puzzle you were trying to put together? The why of it all?"

She nodded as the twinkle of her delight yielded to the curiosity of the detective.

"I'd like to tell you something about that night."

Geez . . . Was Dax involved in Mary's disappearance? Tasha was all ears and all in. "What?"

"I can't know what it are."

"What it are?" She looked through Dax into the past, at the little girl sitting across the table pulling on her ponytail.

"I saw the sorrow in your eyes when you said it, and I felt . . . I feel for you, Tasha. I'd like to help if there's a way."

A far-away look was in her eyes, and I chastised myself for being so direct, which was a fundamental aspect of my nature. I never liked the tango of talking around an issue and preferred a no-nonsense approach to problem solving, a straight line that produced immediate results.

"There's a girl," she said, "a very young girl, who suffered physical, emotional, and sexual abuse by her mother. A mother who rented her out to anyone who paid the price. Twenty dollars for an hour, fifty for the night."

I began to think of how to find that so-called mother. That bitch had to go.

"The mother would take her to a place in the woods where she'd make the little girl . . ." Tasha's eyes shut in an attempt to un-see what she never could – the home movies.

"When I asked Sara if she could help us find the house, she said *I can't know where it are.* It just broke my heart. She barely had a third-grade education."

The agony in her voice made me regret sticking my nose in her business and stirring up her emotions.

"After the mother went to prison, Sara stayed with me until a foster home could be found. She was such a sweet girl, Dax, kind and gentle. Even after everything that had been done to her."

Tears held in place by a seeming strength of will looked ready to let loose, and I laid a hand on her arm, my thumb moving back and forth in a comforting manner. It was an exercise in futility because there was no comfort to be had. But the effort was necessary – for both of us.

"I told her it was over, she'd be safe, and no one else would hurt her. She asked if I promised and I hooked my pinky finger with hers. Over the next three years, against all odds, she became an honor student and was given a ribbon during a school assembly in front of the entire freshman class. The next day, a classmate posted a video he'd found of his father and an eleven-year old Sara. She sent me a note the day she took her life.

*'Sorry, Tasha, but I couldn't find another way.
I looked for an option, an acceptable alternative,
but too many people will see me as that little
girl having sex, and I don't think I can live with
the humiliation. There should be a solution, but
I can't see it or find it or even guess what it
could be. I can't know what it are.'"*

The tears rolled down her cheeks and she looked up at stars blinking off and on through wet eyelashes while suns orbited within galaxies that moved around each other. A confusing cacophony of sight that made it difficult to see your place in the universe or understand a reason for being.

I can't know what it are.

"I let her down. I didn't do enough, didn't . . . I don't know, but I could have done more. I should have."

"What didn't you do?"

Tasha turned on him in frustration, a spark of anger flashing, her fist in a ball and ready to strike. As her fury dissipated, the sincerity of his words resonated, and she considered them from a new perspective.

"You're right. What *could* I have done? How can I keep a thing from happening I have absolutely no control over?"

It was the first time she'd been truly honest with herself without trying to diminish or deflect the truth in favor of her self-imposed castigation.

A measure of blame lifted from her spirit and she wiped the tears from her face with a finger, like a wiper removed rain from a windshield.

"Thanks. I've wrestled with this for a long while, and I appreciate your concern," she said.

I looked into her eyes and saw a wave of friendliness coming my way, ready to break over me with its warmth.

"Dax? Where's Mary?"

~~

'I'll be in your quadrant on Stardate 17713.6. Would like to have lunch in Ten-Forward with a possible visit to Holodeck three. Please confirm. Seven of Nine.'

Jeri sent the text knowing Tasha would respond within ten minutes if she could or by the end of the night if she couldn't. She always smiled when using the show's lexicon to communicate with Tasha, who'd first exposed her to the Star Trek universe years ago at the police academy . . .

        "Your analytical mind along with the ability to contain your emotions is an admirable Borg quality."
    "Borg? What?" Jeri had asked.
    "Star Trek Voyager, tonight at eight. You have cable?"
    "Uh, yeah?"
    "Channel 92. Later, Seven," Tasha said and walked, jogged, and then ran onto the track.
    "Seven? I thought you said it was on at eight?" Jeri shouted at the woman already rounding the first turn.
    That night she'd seen Seven of Nine, an inspirational character who spoke to grace under fire and strength under duress – qualities Jeri would emulate when emotionalism threatened to compromise her reason.
    They'd became fast friends, carefully tending to their friendship even when separated by time and space.

    Jeri shut down the computer and cleared her desk, ready for the long drive home, when the Assistant Deputy-Director called her into his office.
    "Got a couple of minutes, Ryan?"
    "Certainly, sir. Would you like me to sit?"
    "You can if you'd like, but I only have a couple of quick questions. Do you mind?" he asked, reaching for the folder.
    "Not at all, sir. Fire phasers when ready."
    She felt a blush rise from her chest and move upward when he looked at her with a raised eyebrow.
    "Sorry, sir. Star Trek marathon last night," she said as if it were a perfectly acceptable explanation for the breach in decorum. Not that the Deputy-Director was a stickler for protocol. Robert Thompson was a firm but fair boss and treated everyone with respect. Jeri thought the Bureau was lucky to have him.
    "Which series?"

"The Next Generation, sir," she said, the blush in a holding pattern under her chin.

"Miss Ryan. How many times have you called me *Sir* since you stepped into the office?" His face was stoic, but his eyes glimmered as the hue of her cheeks deepened.

"Four, sir. Well, five, now."

"And how many times has that question been asked?" he said and let the grin have its way.

Jeri released the breath she'd been holding and the smile she couldn't contain.

"I know. Sorry. It's a hard habit to break."

"I understand but, in the confines of this office, it's an unnecessary formality."

He opened the folder and scanned the report.

"Do we have sex trade activity down in the Panhandle? I remember we made a few arrests in Panama City last year, but that seemed an isolated incident."

"No, nothing new or known at this time. A detective in St. Vincent asked us to run a possible suspect through our database in regard to a missing father and daughter. I ran all the names and nothing came up."

"What reason did the detective give for thinking," he glanced at the file, "Dax Palmer or John and Mary Stewart might be involved in sex trafficking? What evidence was cited in requesting this enquiry?"

Tasha had sworn her to secrecy about the flash-drive and its contents, and Jeri honored her word in all things where she was concerned. So, she'd tell as much truth as she could without revealing as much as she knew.

"The detective was following a hunch, something that couldn't be corroborated but couldn't be ignored, either."

"It's a bit unusual, isn't it? Using departmental resources with nothing more substantial than a hunch?"

"Yes, sir. But the detective is a good friend of mine, and I've never known her to abuse the resources of any agency. Her reputation is outstanding, her veracity above reproach, and her integrity without question. If she has a hunch, her need is legitimate. I can pull her record, if you'd like."

Thompson raised his hand.

"Your testimonial is more than sufficient, Jeri. If you vouch for her, its good enough for me. Let me know if anything changes in the status of her case. I'm pulling for her, now." He stood and walked around his desk, meeting her as she rose.

"Miss Ryan. Just one more question."

"Yes?"

"Kirk, Picard, or Janeway?"

Jeri's eyes lit up and her face broke into a smile.

"Sir, don't get me started."

~~

Where's Mary??

The expected warm wave of affection crashed over me with an icy chill. I was totally unprepared for the question and completely dependent upon my automatic response to unexpected stimuli – absolute calm.

Which I was *not*.

In an instant, my brain offered three explanations for her question – she knew, she suspected, she was being rhetorical. I went with rhetorical.

She wasn't asking me specifically but metaphorically: me, herself, the universe – where's Mary? Where could she be, what happened to her? She didn't really think I knew where she was.

Did she?

"I'm sorry, Tasha. I wish I could tell you."

"What?"

She'd tuned out, thinking about Mary and hoping to find her before she made a similar choice to the one Sara made. The girl she'd seen on those videos couldn't have survived much longer. Not six months, not six weeks, perhaps not even six days. She might already be dead.

"Sorry Dax. I was lost in my thoughts. I'm worried about Mary Stewart. I need to find her. Before . . ."

Her eyes were grey-black. I moved closer and gently placed my hand on her back. Tasha leaned into me and the storm cloud broke. She didn't sob or make any noise, just let the tears flow unimpeded without any effort to contain them. I patted and move my hand up and down, trying to ease her pain, soothe her spirit, be her friend.

I didn't think the tears were only about Mary, but I believed Tasha saw her as a soul to be saved and not just another case to be solved. She cared about her.

I could relate.

"Thanks," she said as she moved away and dried her eyes. Other than Jeri, she hadn't felt close to anyone. She'd question and analyze the reasons later, but she was grateful for the care Dax gave and her sadness diminished.

"I don't know why I've been so emotional tonight. Maybe it's the alcohol. Probably has something to do with it, but it's more than that. I've been carrying around a lot of ... weight. For a long time, now. I think you've helped lift some of that, though I'm at a loss as to how. But Dax, I'm thankful. Truly."

She reached out her hand and I took it, but instead of shaking them, we held on instead. I began to consider how Mary and I might approach her when a chirping noise made me grin.

"Was that the sound of a communicator opening?"

She laughed, took the phone from her bag, and nodded. "It's Seven of Nine. She wants to have lunch in Ten-Forward, maybe go to Holodeck three afterward."

I raised my brow and grinned as she explained.

chapter thirteen

He had to be dead.

If his brother were alive he would have kept in touch, kept showing him what he was doing to her and rubbing it in his face. Even if he'd disposed of her, he wouldn't have gone so long without contacting him; in fact, he would have called right away asking for his help. What puzzled him was why anyone would have killed him?

James moved the cursor on the mousepad, clicked on the button, and started the video. She was sleek, graceful, seductive, and enthusiastic in pursuing her pleasure.

John's right, he thought, watching his niece climax. That moan was extraordinary and the fullness of it always stirred something inside of him, something deep. She'd be worth a small fortune on the black market.

Maybe that's it? John could have said something to someone and showed her to the wrong people.

Well, we're all the wrong people, James chuckled, but he meant the ones who'd just kill you and take your property - wham, bam, fuck you, man.

He'd advised his brother to sell her to a buyer overseas, but John had been reluctant, saying she'd come around and when she did, he'd have her completely and for years.

John wasn't stupid, but he was impulsive. What he did to his daughter was an example, and he'd put himself in an untenable position. He couldn't keep her tied up forever. Then a video arrived with a note – 'Ha-ha. Look what I got. Told you she wanted it.'

After seeing the way Mary gave herself to him, James developed an itch he'd wanted to scratch. But John refused.

'Hell no, brother-mine. This is as close as your gonna get to my little girl. You've got one of your own.'

Which was ridiculous. He could never do that to Jewels – not without extensive planning and significant risk. Unlike John, he had a wife and two other children, as well as a job that took up a significant amount of his time.

However, the thought began to take root the first time he watched Mary ride his brother on a flower decaled bed.

After she rolled over and offered herself on hands and knees, James imagined himself in John's place as he mauled her breasts and pounded her from behind. But the impetus of his own daughter's destruction came when Mary lifted her head and stared right at him. The expression on her face exhilarated, but the look in her eyes electrified.

James had only seen that look once a long time ago in his childhood, the day he heard a noise coming from the backroom bedroom. His mother's . . .

He'd pressed an ear against the smooth wooden door, turning the knob in his hand. He didn't hear him hitting her, but she groaned all the same.

His stepfather had always told him and his brother to knock on that door and wait – or else, but James' curiosity nudged it open a crack and he saw him kneeled behind her with his eyes closed, holding on as she made her sounds and pushed against the mattress.

She saw him through the sliver of open door when she lifted her head, and he should have turned and run. But what held him there, mesmerized and aroused, was the look in his sister's eyes as she watched him watch her.

It changed him in a fundamental way, but he didn't know why or what it meant.

It was about dominion.

Ownership gave the right to impose oneself on another, to force them into submission until they gave themselves physically, emotionally, and most importantly, sexually.

James had exerted that power over many daughters of other fathers and enjoyed the many pleasures they'd given. But it never equaled the ecstasy he'd shared with his sister.

Maybe it was because he'd been so young.? Or perhaps the familial connection was the most powerful expression of that authority, the carnality that created the euphoria?

The realization was almost an epiphany.

My father, his daughter. My brother, his. Mine . . .

James powered down the laptop and sat with his hands steepled against his lips, contemplating the evil in the world and his part in it. Jewels always brought a smile to his face, her humor was engaging, and her innocence a delight. He'd never had a single thought about her that put her at risk.

Until he saw that look in Mary's eyes.

"Daddy?" she said, knocking on the door.

"Come in, honey."

~~

"Don't stop."

Mary's breath quickened as she rolled Dax over and straddled him, her hair disheveled, her hands grasping, her legs squeezing, her breasts heaving against his chest, her face inches from his and looking into eyes that wanted her – to smash the bridge of his nose with her forehead.

Or bite it hard, if necessary.

"Ok, I get it," she said, standing and giving him a hand up. She grabbed a towel and wiped her face, pulling her hair back and returning it to the confines of the scrunchie.

"The important thing to remember is – never stop fighting. Unless it's a ruse to improve your situation. I like how you used your legs to squeeze my sides when I grabbed your hands. That was a good move given your limited attack options. It put more pressure on me and added to your upcoming head-butt. You did good, kid. Except..."

"Who you calling kid?"

She flicked the towel and saw it snap where his leg was before it wasn't. "And what do you mean, except?"

I'd seen that towel coming in the glint of her eye long before it left her hand and had moved to avoid its sting. I stuck my tongue out at her and she reciprocated.

"I thought you had a chance to get a knee between my legs before you rolled on top of me. Could have shortened the struggle, maybe, with a hard-driven knee to the crotch. Yes?"

Mary nodded and looked behind me, startled. Half-way into my turn to see, I saw the reason when her towel found its mark on my backside. I snatched the terrycloth in a flash, and her *Ha* of glee change to an *Ah* of surprise when I grabbed ahold of her wrist, turned her around, and put her in a choke hold.

She raised her left leg without hesitation and stomped her foot on my own just above the ankle – then brought the heel of her right foot up between my legs. I barely caught it with my thighs before she bent forward and pulled me off balance, pushed off with her free foot, and let my body absorb the shock and sudden impact of the floor behind me.

My grip loosened, and she drove an elbow into my side and rolled away before I could grab her hair to pull her back. She stood just outside my reach in a fighting stance watching every move I made, daring me to continue.

"And what, exactly, will you do if I do?"

"Kick or stomp your head," she said. "Maybe drive my knee into your face, or my fist or elbow into your eye. Maybe stick my thumbs into both of them till you stop or put you in a choke hold of my own."

I noted her confidence as beads of sweat dripped from her brow, silhouetted by a glow of satisfaction in her eyes. She'd be a physical force to be reckoned with someday, a perfect complement to her intellectual prowess.

"And what, exactly, would you do if I didn't?"

"Huh?" The towel hung over her shoulder, and she wiped her forehead with the end of it.

I leaned on my side, trying not to aggravate the muscle her elbow had found. We'd only been training at about sixty percent, but my throbbing ankle said it was closer to ninety.

"If I *didn't* move. Didn't give you a reason to react. What would you do?"

Mary thought about it and looked at me curiously. "That's a good question. It's relative, isn't it?"

"Yes. Very good. It *is* relative. To your surroundings, to your strengths, to your opponent's, to the circumstances.

With so many variables to be factored, it's imperative to keep one thing in mind – do what has to be done. And even more importantly – *do what has to be done.* Understand?"

She nodded her head, shook it, and then raised a brow in confusion. "You've got some 'splainin' to do, Lucy."

I smiled at her paraphrased impression and took pride in her ability to use applicable movie and television quotes and lingo in everyday sass and situations. She got that from me, and it reinforced my belief of being a positive influence in her life.

"If anyone tries to intimidate, confront, bully, badger, bother, hassle, or in any way hurt you or anyone you want to protect, don't wait to retaliate. If they are close enough to do you harm, put them down quickly and harshly. So far, so good?"

Mary nodded, understanding the meaning and purpose of what Dax was saying – immediately address the threat before it escalated into a more dangerous situation.

"If they're vulnerable, like I was, and they continue to attack, do what has to be done. Like you were going to do. Like you were ready to do. Can I get an amen?"

She smiled and put her hands in the air.

"Amen and hallelujah, brother. Preach it."

As much as I loved her, which was deeply and forever, I liked her even more. She was off the like-o-meter chart.

"But Mare. If someone tries to take you, subdue you, endanger you, or kill you, and they're down and vulnerable? Do not hesitate to do what has to be done. You kill them. Immediately and permanently."

I could see the struggle within her, the intellectual and the emotional, the right and the wrong, the little girl and the one she'd become. What I couldn't see was the certainty of what she'd do. I got up and put my hand on her shoulder.

"Otherwise, they will live to take, subdue, endanger, or kill another day. You or someone else. And honey, if something happens to you, it's going to hurt me."

Her eyes softened, and she nodded.

"Well, at least for a day or two," I said. "Then I'd be okay, I think."

I bent down to grab the old wrestling mat we used and saw the glint in her eye as she took and twirled the towel.

Mary whistled a tune as she left to take a shower, and I waited until she closed her door before rubbing my bottom. *Damn, that hurt.*

I rolled the mat up and against the wall. I'd found it on Craigslist shortly after she came to live with me and had cut it to fit the large room I previously used as a storage, throw crap-in, kind of space. Cleaning it up had taken almost a day.

The room faced the back yard, so I'd rigged alarms to sound whenever a vehicle first pulled into the driveway, then half-way down the two hundred-yard length of it, and finally, within a hundred feet of the house.

Three different warnings for distance and redundancy. We didn't want anyone to sneak up on us, especially when we were training or playing music.

The sky is crying . . .

Oh shit!! The doorbell.

I rushed to Mary's room and knocked, and then entered when she didn't answer, ran past her bed to the bathroom and knocked again. The shower was running, and a cloud of steam escaped when I opened the door enough to be heard.

"Mary. Code red."

"What? How . . . Okay."

The sky is crying. . .

I scrambled through her room, heard the shower stop, picked the towel off the floor, and threw it over my shoulder on the way. After locking her bedroom, I looked out the front door peephole and opened it after the second knock, pleased and perplexed.

"Hey, Tasha. Whatchu up to, girlfriend?" I snapped my fingers as my hand moved back and forth across my body.

She fell out, and the emerald qualities of her hazel-green eyes twinkled with tears of merriment. Her response cracked *me* up, and we were soon laughing well above the market value of my levity futures.

"I don't know why that was so funny Dax, but damned if it wasn't. Are you a comedian, as well as a musician?" she asked, wiping the tears from her eyes.

"Oh yeah. I'm the funniest person this side of the door. In fact, I play to a full house every time a delivery guy or girl comes to the porch. They usually ask for my autograph, so I must be pretty good," I said with an eyebrow and nod that acknowledged my *specialness.*

"No, stop," she said and started to giggle.

Her efforts to contain her hilarity were hindered by my look of wide-eyed belief in my exceptionalism. When my expression changed from one of confidence to confusion and then wounded, my eyes puppy-dogged as I shook my head and finger-snapped my hand again, looking pitiful.

Tasha cried from laughter, bouncing anxiously from one foot to the other.

"Dax, no. I can't. I'm going to . . ."

She looked behind me, around me, and into me. I told her where to find it and peered outside as she raced down the hallway. This was a potentially dangerous situation with only myself to blame.

Was I really that funny?

I sat in the big chair, my brain whirring with worry, and contemplated the suddenness of the wolf at my door, now in my bathroom. I patted the towel on my face and began to lower my heart rate with slow, deliberate breaths, moving toward my go-to state of mind – cold, calculating calm.

~~

Jeri Ryan sat waiting in Hartsfield-Jackson for a flight to Northwest Florida Beaches International airport.

She'd meet with officials in Panama City and Panama City Beach this morning, and with Tasha this afternoon for lunch at Spinnaker's Paradise Grill, *Ten-Forward* in Star Trek parlance. The food was good and the view even better.

Jeri would sit on the beach the rest of the day and into the night if she could, letting her toes sink into the sand as the saltwater washed away the cares of her world. But she needed to be at work early tomorrow and wouldn't be able to enjoy the nightlife of music and dancing with Tasha in *Holodeck three* – Spinnaker's Beach Club.

They used to spend some time at Club La Vela next door, billed as the largest nightclub in the United States, but now preferred the less rambunctious crowds at Spinnaker. The people there could get rowdy too, but the decibel level was far below that of La Vela's.

Jeri would send Tasha a text after boarding the plane to let her know she was on her way. She'd been missing her more than usual lately and was looking forward to laughing and catching up with her best friend.

~~

Ask not for whom the toilet flushes, I thought and smiled as water ran in the sink, glad to know she washed her hands. Tasha's time in the bathroom was brief but long enough to open the medicine cabinet and other doors and drawers.

I'm not saying she did, just that she could have.

Which was why I'd given Mary the master bedroom with its own facilities. She never used the other one, so there wasn't anything for Tasha to find. We'd discussed the possibility of someone else using that bathroom but hadn't expected that someone to be the detective looking for her.

I got up from the chair and went into the kitchen, pulled two mugs from the freezer and poured a couple of cold ones.

"Dax?"

"In the kitchen. I'll be right out. My workout made me thirsty, and you look like you're off duty, so I thought a cold beer might hit the spot."

"Dax, I appreciate that, but I'm driving to Panama City and . . . Wait. I thought you didn't like beer?"

Her eyes widened when she saw the large, frosty mugs.

"No way. Come on. How did you know? How could you?" A look of amazement sparked in her eyes, and a spontaneously combusted smile lit her face.

Damn. She sure was pretty.

"I read your mind the other night when you were gazing at the night sky. Hope that's alright?" I set the tray on the coffee table and invited her to sit and drink.

My fondness for her began when she plopped into the big chair – *my* chair, grabbed a mug, and emptied it in one long drink. A foam mustache sat on an upper lip that curled at the corners as she set the glass down, eyed the full one beside it, and then looked at me with a question in her eyes.

I nodded and took both tray and empty to the kitchen, returning with two more ice-cold mugs of A&W. She sat rocking and sipping her rootbeer, grinning and looking like a little girl. I hoped my own was holding up alright.

After taking a mug, I pushed the tray toward her and sat on the couch. She shook her head and said, "I can't."

"Sure you can. Just get it before I finish mine, or you'll have to arm wrestle me for it."

She swapped out the empty for the full, and we talked about our love of A&W rootbeer, her friend coming to Florida, and a friend of mine who'd recently left the state.

"This is a great chair, Dax. It's like an amusement park ride," she said, putting it through its rocking, reclining, tilting, swiveling paces. After the second spin around, she stopped and stared.

"Is that a Martin D-28?"

She walked over to the guitar and looked back at me.

"Go ahead," I said in my best Clint Eastwood voice. "Make my day."

Tasha grinned and picked up the guitar with respect and reverence, sat on the stool, strummed an E chord, and closed her eyes as the strings rang loud and clear. She began to fingerpick an intricate melody over a familiar chord pattern leading to the beginning of one of my favorite songs.

"Summertime . . ."

Man, what a voice.

I already had goosebumps and went to accompany her with the Epiphone. Tasha didn't open her eyes till the second verse, and, when she did, her love of music was evident. I knew Mary could hear us and wondered what she was thinking. She'd love to be part of this.

Tasha let me have a solo and seemed to like the bluesy style I was playing but gave a look when I rocked it up a bit. I attacked the strings, my face a scrunched-up, tuned in, far out expression of rock and roll angst. She stopped playing long before I realized she had.

"What the heck? This ain't no Rockstar moment," she said with a grin and shake of her head. "Lead guitarists. Give them an inch and they'll take the whole damned song."

~~

Watson walked in from the backyard and stopped when he saw the two of them. Before he could slip back outside, the lady smiled. Ever the courteous canine, Watson tipped his head and glanced at Dax, who looked as surprised as he was.

"Come here, boy."

Boy? Watson walked on over.

"What's his name? He's a cutie pie."

He cocked his head. *Cutie pie?*

"Doug."

Watson looked at Dax with incredulity.

"Doug? You don't hear that name very often, do you? But, he's pretty darn cute. Aren't you, boy?"

Listen. I am not a boy. I'm a well read, full grown . . .

She scratched his head and cheeks, spending some time behind his ears. "How long have you had him?"

I told her I'd found him at the house one day after coming home from a trip, and he'd been with me ever since – which was true, and if she didn't ask for elaboration, I wouldn't have to lie to her about when and why he'd come. I didn't want to start a friendship based on lies. Deceptions and half-truths maybe, but not lies.

Watson had tuned out of the conversation the moment the lady found a spot adjacent to *the* spot. He tried to maneuver her fingers into position, but she moved around. The scratching was good enough, however, to cloud his judgement as he left for Mary's room.

"Hey, Doug," I called out, trying to prevent the curiosity that would come from a dog sitting in front of a closed door, or worse, asking Mary to let him in.

"Douglas?"

Watson stopped and looked back with embarrassment on his face and an apology in his eye.

"Don't you want your Snausages before you take your mid-morning nap?" I asked.

Watson smiled, nodded, and walked to the kitchen.

"Huh," Tasha said, after I'd followed him in.

"What?"

I spoke a little louder so she could hear me and opened the pantry door, coming out with three treats that Watson inhaled as I rubbed him up and patted him down.

"He looked like he nodded when you asked about the Snausages."

"Really?" I raised an eyebrow and he nodded.

"Yeah. And I could have sworn I saw him smile."

"Huh." I grinned at him and he winked.

The Star Trek communicator ringtone I'd heard the other night asked to be acknowledged.

"That your friend?" I asked, walking into the room and sending Watson outside. Tasha was reading a text. If her smile was any indication, she liked her friend very much.

"Yes," she said, putting the phone in her purse and the strap over her shoulder.

The Martin stood on the guitar stand, and I wished I'd recorded her. Maybe next time.

Next time? *Next* time? How many chances was I going to give her to find Mary? What was I thinking letting Tasha in the house in the first place?

Why was *I so damned funny?*

"Dax, this has been an unexpected delight. You can't know how much I've needed something like this. Or maybe you can? I came over to thank you for the consideration and care you gave me the other night. It meant something, and I appreciate it. I appreciate you."

I was touched and moved and concerned. Trying to be a friend had put everything at risk.

Why was *I so damned caring?*

"Well, thanks, Tasha. It meant something to me, too."

We looked at each other, and she moved closer.

"Dax. Would it be okay if I . . .?"

I raised my eyebrow and she nodded.

"Sure, girlfriend," I said, snapping my finger with flair. "You know where it is."

She giggled and walked quickly to the bathroom.

I waited two minutes after Tasha left before knocking on her door with the *all clear* signal – one knock, two knocks with a hesitation before a third, and then three final knocks. I went inside when she didn't respond.

"Mary. It's clear."

The bathroom door opened and it was all I could do to stifle a laugh. She stood wrapped in a towel with dried soap on her arms, legs, and face. There was a glob of shampoo in her hair, and a look in her eyes that was angry and cute at the same time. She was precious.

"Oh, sweetie."

"Don't *Oh, sweetie* me, Dax. I was in there, not moving, not wiping the soap off me, not sneezing, not coughing, not doing anything, a-n-y-t-h-i-n-g, that would make noise or draw attention, while you were laughing and drinking and singing and playing my guitar for what, thirty minutes?"

"Actually, forty-one, plus the two I waited after she left. But seriously, Mare, I am so proud of you for following emergency protocols to the letter."

"Don't *Mare* me, either. And stop smiling. I'll take you to the mat right now and give you a hundred percent of kick-ass if you don't wipe the smile off your face."

She started to grin in spite of herself, causing me to upgrade my smile to an ill-advised chuckle.

"Oohhh, don't even," she said, trading her grin for a grimace and surprising me with her speed.

I barely reached the hall in time to close the door and hold on to the knob for dear life while she pulled and banged and shouted and giggled, laughed, and squealed.

God, I loved that kid.

chapter fourteen

Tasha turned right off Thomas Drive and drove up the Hathaway Bridge over the waters of the Upper Grand Lagoon connecting Panama City Beach with Panama City.

She loved the bridge.

The vista of bridge, buildings, boats, and what she called 'big bayou' water, was a soothing sight and always replenished her soul. It symbolized the possibility of people – to imagine, to create, to build, to overcome. To work together for the common good instead of the destructive pursuit of selfishness.

She smiled as a melody raised her spirit. Some might think that's a lot of meaning attached to one edifice but – *all she was saaayying, was give bridge a chance.*

Tasha beeped the horn, stuck her hand out the window, and waved as she turned for St. Vincent and home. Jeri flashed her lights, beeping back as she headed to the airport. Tasha already missed her; their time together too brief.

We should take another vacation. It had been six years since Acapulco, and they'd had a blast. Sun, sand, water, and drink by day, with more of the same on warm balmy nights. They'd played music, chess, cards, smoked cigars and sang in the local bar for free fruity, liquor-laden beverages.

Tasha thought about her friend's reaction to her recounting of the last few days . . .

"Wait, what? Are you saying Dax isn't a suspect now? The database search wasn't necessary?" Jeri had asked.

"Yes, no. Wait. No, Dax isn't a suspect. And yes, the search was necessary because of the flash-drive videos. The father is still the primary suspect in his daughter's disappearance. He raped her. I know it, and her having sex with him doesn't change that. Her will was broken. You can see it in her eyes. She hated what she was doing, even though it appears otherwise. I believe that."

Jeri nodded.

"Perhaps you could turn the flash-drive over anyway? Might be enough to reopen the case. Or, more accurately,, to *open* a case."

While the sudden departure of the Stewart's was suspicious, an official case had never been opened because there wasn't any evidence of foul play, no blood or signs of struggle in or around the house, nothing to suggest anything other than a family taking off for reasons of their own.

Her captain couldn't justify the time, manpower, and expense to investigate a mystery, and Tasha had agreed. Until she found the flash-drive. Till she'd seen what that father was doing to his child.

"I don't know, Seven. I'm not sure turning it in would make it better for that girl. In fact, it might make it worse. Sure, he would be arrested for having sexual relations with a child, and maybe he'd get the maximum sentence. But I seriously doubt it. Those videos show a girl who seems to know what she's doing, and I think some jurors will dismiss the psychology in favor of the sexuality. It's more . . . titillating."

"True dat," Jeri said, nodding her head with a glimmer in her eye and making Tasha chuckle.

"True dat? What, are you hip now? Or hop?"

"I am all things cool and happening."

Maybe Jeri is why I like Dax so much, Tasha thought. They both had the same humor and quick-witted replies.

"But even if the world all of a sudden grew up and grew a pair and sent that son of a bitch to the electric chair or, better yet, to jail for the rest of his life with men using him five times a day – think about that girl? About people knowing her story, how they'd look at her, what they'd say." Tasha said, looking away as her voice softened.

"Maybe she's strong enough to survive the horror of her story. Maybe. Maybe not. She might kill herself the moment someone knows. Or hang on and try to build a life – until a video surfaces."

Her eyes watered, and Jeri placed a hand over her friend's. She knew Tasha was thinking about Sara, the little girl who'd killed herself just as her future began.

"It's a crap shoot, Jeri, and I don't want to roll the dice. If she's out there somewhere trying to escape the evil of her father and somehow manages to overcome the torment and humiliation of her experience, I can't let those videos harm her. I can't. I won't," she said with conviction.

Jeri patted her hand with affection and understanding. "I completely agree. The girl's safety is the overriding consideration. It trumps everything. Including the law. I gotchu, girlfriend," she added with a snap of her fingers.

Tasha laughed. Hard. Gut wrenching, table slapping, tears running down her cheeks hard. Jeri's look of confusion intensified her laughter, and it took a long few minutes before Tasha could explain.

"Dax sounds interesting. Maybe even a little bit cool. Looks like you've made a new friend. You okay with it?"

"Yeah. Maybe. How about you? *You* okay with it?"

"Well, you seem to be having fun, so I like that. And you laugh like you mean it, so I like that, too. I suppose there are two areas of concern, things I'd need to know."

Tasha raised her brow.

"First, am I still your girl?"

"You will always be my girl, Seven. As I will always be yours." Tasha put a hand on her best friend's and squeezed, her eyes filled with love and sincerity.

Jeri smiled and nodded. "Second, and more important . . . Am I funnier than Dax?"

~~

I turned from the mailbox and watched the sun fall below the horizon. It was disappointing. I had yet to see the green light people said blinked at the exact moment the sun disappeared. For years, I've looked for that singular flash of brilliance, and what had I gotten instead? Skies of red and yellow and purple and pink and gold and . . .

Well, you get the multi-colored picture.

I checked connections on each of the electronic eyes for loose or broken wires on my walk up the driveway, trying to track down the reason my fail-safe, triple redundancy alarm and warning system had failed. Everything looked good, and I suspected the problem was with the remote.

Or more specifically, the remote operator.

I'd forgotten to put batteries back in it after borrowing them for the garage remote – whose batteries I'd borrowed to turn on the television. While this was an unacceptable level of incompetence, it was all kinds of funny.

Of course, the funny was relative. Made possible by Mary being here and safe instead of taken away and at risk. It would be unbearable to sit in a jail cell and be unable to help her if she needed me. I couldn't trust the police to do right by her, to protect and love her.

That was *my* job.

As I left the mailbox and walked down the driveway, the individual alarms triggered. In addition to giving an internal audible warning, the alarms caused a green, yellow, or red light to flash in the house. I saw the red one blink through a window and made a mental note to keep that curtain drawn.

Can't let visitors know we know they're coming, right?

One of the limitations of this system was its efficiency in detecting every moving thing – coyotes, bears, birds, raccoons, armadillos. The 'eyes' were raised to eliminate smaller animals and I could only monitor the driveway, not the woods on either side. Now, only vehicles and people triggered the alarm, as well as deer, bear, and the occasional freakishly long-legged blue heron. There was a lizard, once.

Of course, anyone who knew about the alarms could easily walk around them and remain undetected till they knocked on the door. Or rang the doorbell like Tasha had.

The motion detectors lights lit the way as I walked the perimeter of the house before going into the garage and closing the door – manually.

I needed to buy some batteries.

~~

Kevin checked the time and recorded it in the notepad. He kept filming the house for another couple of minutes, although there wasn't anything more to see. The curtains were closed. He'd positioned himself optimally, recording the back and forth trip up the driveway, and he would stay in place for another hour, at least

Or until a snake slithered by.

The pay was good and the risk low, but he wasn't sharing any space with any snake.

~~

Mary watched herself make another drink.

She had become adept at minimizing the taste of the liquor, which was necessary because the girl needed more and more alcohol as she gave herself over and over.

That girl thought about running away all the time, despising what she was doing. But Mary knew he'd kill her the moment he doubted her desire for him. So she waited for her best chance, a time she'd be alone and unrestrained.

Mary knew the girl couldn't hold on much longer. Even if her plan succeeded, she would always be tormented by the things she'd done to facilitate her escape.

But as she watched the girl suffer her humiliation, she saw the reason for it from a perspective she'd never thought possible: absolute truth, free of judgement. After months of self-condemnation, Mary now understood – she'd had no control over what happened, none whatsoever. It was him, and it was always going to be him who was to blame. He bore all of the responsibility for having to save herself . . . however she could.

She wished she could tell the girl there was hope and peace beyond the nightmare of her existence, that someone was waiting to love her, someone who'd strengthen and encourage her to believe in herself. Someone she didn't know existed but now couldn't live without.

Hang on, Mary. Soon you'll be free, and he'll be dead.

She spread her arms and rose into the sky, flying for the first time since the forest night.

~~

Tasha sat in bed with her back against the headboard, a computer on her lap. She clicked pause and tried to wipe the fatigue from her eyes, determined to go through the videos one last time.

She'd been looking at each one in detail, and, while not yet finding a clue that might lead to her whereabouts, she had gained some insight into Mary.

The videos of her alone and in the privacy of her room showed a confident young lady, one comfortable with her body and herself. Her eyes, though engaged in her activity, revealed a sweet innocent delight that Tasha recognized because she'd felt the same before that day in the library – Mary loved herself and her life.

But that innocence was in stark contrast to glimpses of despair visible when she was with her father. They were brief and sometimes subtle, and you'd miss them if you didn't know what you were seeing, if you were watching her body instead and what she was doing – because what she was doing looked freely given.

But that was a lie, and Tasha had known it long before she saw Mary on her hands and knees, before she'd looked up at her. Overwhelmed with compassion, she had paused the video and touched the face of a little girl running out of hope, unaware anyone could see her pain or ever would.

That little girl wasn't consenting but complying, her choices limited or non-existent. Tasha knew it in her bones. But what she knew she couldn't prove, and that's why she hadn't turned in the flash-drive. And why she'd destroy it. She couldn't trust others to see what she had. Not the captain, or the state's attorney. Maybe not even Dominic.

She rubbed the back of her neck, moved her head from side to side, pushed play to resume her search, and saw John Stewart sitting on the couch with Mary sitting on his lap. After a few minutes, she started to fast forward through what they were doing when something caught her eye.

Mary had leaned back, and, in the open space between them, Tasha saw the headstock and fretboard of a guitar, probably an acoustic given the width of the board. She thought it similar to the one she'd played at Dax's this morning. The color looked the same, but, as she enlarged the picture, the pixel resolution grew worse.

114

Tasha hesitated to erase Mary's videos before taking it out back and taking a hammer to it. She teared up, knowing it needed to be done but feeling like she'd lose her somehow if she did. When she clicked Enter to format the flash-drive, the tears tumbled, followed by many more.

As she finally began to sleep, a thought formed but didn't inform, deciding rather to let her rest. Besides, it had heard through the synapse about a costume party being held in the frontal lobe, and it wanted to attend, perhaps going as a bright idea. It did leave her a note, however.

'I didn't see that guitar when I searched the house.'

~~

Watson and Mary had been asleep for an hour. I didn't want to wake them by rocking, so I leaned back in the big chair. After a few deep breaths, I was ready.

Mary hadn't said much about Tasha coming to see me or what it might mean. She said she trusted my judgement, and the way she'd looked at me lifted my spirit and made me afraid – because a decision needed to be made, and, more than that, it needed to be implemented. And with its implementation, the consequences would ensue.

Tasha had become a dilemma of my own making. I could have left her alone with her grief, given her cleverness instead of compassion, concoctions instead of comfort, or just plain not liked her.

I could have been less damned funny.

When she left this morning, I knew I'd found a friend. Someone I cared about and invited to care about me. It would be difficult, now, to give a satisfactory explanation for moving to the cabin. And more difficult still, to pretend she was only a casual acquaintance.

Tasha was too perceptive to believe that. She'd also be curious, or suspicious, about why I got involved in her personal life and then left town. And, of course, she could just show up at the cabin; the chance of discovery there being the same as here.

I saw two options, both risky because we'd have to do one or the other right away before she found Mary.

One - We pack the van and leave.

I'd tell Tasha I was taking a trip north through Canada, a six-week excursion I'd been planning for months. Mary and I would then head west after trading the van for a motorhome in Indiana. We'd stay on the road a while, be cognizant and careful, and then find a place somewhere and settle back down.

It would be an adventure, one she'd probably enjoy.

Two - Mary and I sit down with Tasha.

Not the Chief of Police, not the State's Attorney, but Tasha. She cared about Mary and would be sensitive and supportive. Even more so after seeing the videos.

But as I considered this option, I quickly dismissed it. If the videos the police had showed Mary participating, she'd have to explain her actions to others who might judge. The full extent of what that would do to her I couldn't know, but I wasn't willing to risk it. She was in a good place now, with her whole life ahead.

After getting up and going to the fridge, I poured some ice-cold water, turned off the backyard motion sensors, and sat outside in the dark. I took a long drink and stared at the couch through the window, the one I put her on the night I'd found her. The night I found myself.

I began to plan our escape.

chapter fifteen

James admired the curvature of her bottom as she bent over to pick up the ball. He was appreciative of her body and liked the sleek line from slender hips and tiny waist to pert, burgeoning breasts. He took a deep breath and slowly exhaled, remembering another young girl from long ago . . .

"Are you sure about this, James? She looks scared."

"I know. Isn't it great?"

John had to admit it was exciting to watch her struggle. Her underwear was stuffed in her mouth, and her naked body glistened as the moonlight peered through the broken window. He reached for her breast and pinched and pulled, softly at first and then harder as she squirmed in pain or pleasure, John didn't know which.

But her groans stimulated a craving.

Earlier, when he'd asked where he was sneaking off to, James said an older girl was *wet and waiting* in the woods, that she'd teased him at school and said she wanted to *do it*. James had invited him along – if he wasn't *too chicken*.

John might not have believed his brother except he'd heard whispers in class about the things she'd been doing. But that was with boys much older than them.

Soon after James left, John worked up the courage and crawled out the window, tiptoed across the roof, and climbed down the ivy trellis at the back of the house.

He hurried through the trees to the worn-down shack and then crept to the broken window. James had a hand behind her head as she knelt on the floor, and winked when he glanced over and saw him watching. John smiled back and felt a strange sensation that made him fidget.

She stood up and tried to kiss him on the lips, but James told her to take her panties off and go sit on the table. She acted surprised but did what he said, and John thought she probably wasn't used to a boy their age being so bossy.

James had become very aggressive since spending time alone with their father and sister. When John asked what they were doing, his brother always smiled and said he'd show him one day.

The girl kissed his neck as James spread open her legs and fondled her before he stepped between and against her.

John watched his brother push and push, and a hunger he hadn't known asked to be fed when the girl threw her head back and made a sound similar to the one he'd make when the first bite of chocolate cake exploded on his tongue – but much more intense. John didn't know exactly what he was doing to her, but he wanted to do it too.

James took off her shirt, pulled her up, turned her around, and bent her over the table until she was face down. Her arms were by her side, and she grasped the edge of the tabletop as he pressed and pushed from behind, making her pant and groan. He slid off his belt, looped and tightened it around her wrists, and then stepped back.

"Ooohh, don't stop, kid. You're doing great," she said, looking around for him. She saw a boy at the window as her head yanked back and something was shoved in her mouth. The soft material muffled her words and screams.

After removing the skirt, James sat her on the edge, grabbed a handful, and walked around the table, pulling her by the hair until she lay in the middle, splayed and ready.

"Come on in, brother-mine. Let's have some fun. Time to show you what you've been wanting to know."

They did everything to her they could think of, taking her over and over and over.

Ah, the stamina of youth, James thought, watching Jewels throw the ball back to the twins. That night in the cabin was a fond memory, but it had cost him time and loss.

The girl had a reputation as the school slut, so no one believed she'd been forced into anything, certainly not raped. But the attention drawn to the brothers caused their parents to send them away to separate boarding schools thousands of miles apart. He suspected his mother was trying to protect John, thinking James had led his younger brother astray. But John wanted what he'd done to that girl. He told him.

It was seventeen years before he saw his brother again, and they picked up where they'd left off, with a new girl every few months. Until, against his persistent warnings, John gave in to his craving and fed his daughter to the beast.

I miss you, brother.

James thought about his sister and his time with her. He'd meant to go back, but she'd killed their step-father on a cold October afternoon before swallowing the gun herself.

I miss you, sister.

One of the boys threw the ball over her head, and he watched Jewels run to pick it up again. His mind slowed her movement, the fluid motion of her body, and the back and forth swing of her ponytail. He imagined his hand wrapped tightly around it.

~~

The cornerstone of my relationship with Mary was honesty. We had a deal – whatever asked, we told the truth. Or respectfully declined to answer. And while a *respectfully declined* yes or no question couldn't be confirmed, it could nevertheless be inferred.

'Did you use a coaster under your drink last night?'

I respectfully decline to answer.

'Have you been going outside in the daytime?'

I plead the fifth. When I asked if she even knew what the fifth was, she said *one more than the fourth.*

When it came to *telling* each other things, however, it was different. There were omissions of truth, at least on my part, and, to Mary's credit, she didn't ask me about many of the things I did or look *into me* to get the answers.

I'd told her I was hauling a few things out to the cabin to prepare for our probable move and would make another trip or two before we left, which was true. The van was loaded with stuff, and I was indeed on my way to drop it off. But, I didn't mention the move would be cross country.

Before leaving town, I stopped by the bank to withdraw money split evenly between traveler's checks and cash, as well as transferring dollars to other accounts at different institutions. I'd worked out a tentative plan based on both static and dynamic circumstances.

Assuming I wasn't a suspect in Mary's disappearance, I'd drain those accounts over the six weeks I was in 'Canada.'

But you know what happens when you *ass u me* . . .

So, at the first sign of trouble, I'd leave that money be and use the cash I had stashed. Don't bother asking where or how I got it because I'm not telling.

After unloading the van, I checked the deer cameras peppered around the property. They could record, notify when activated. or watch in real time. It was my intention to move as much as I could from the house to the cabin for safe keeping before we left the state.

It might not look it, but the structure was solidly built, with steel curtains and doors, and a panic room underneath that wasn't on any floor plan. It was miles from town and neighbors, with room to roam and woods to conceal.

Mary and I might have stayed there for a long while. Yes, I could discourage Tasha from coming to the Cove or my house, act like I wasn't interested in her friendship, pretend I didn't really care about her and carefully move into the cabin and out of her jurisdiction.

I could do all of those things, except . . . I couldn't.

How could I hurt her like that after drawing her out and sharing her pain? Especially after seeing her suffer because of Sara and Mary?

So, I'd disappear on my fake Canadian trip and leave her with another mystery, another person she'd try to find but never would – and end up hurting her anyway.

I checked the home mailbox and pressed the button to let Mary know it was me coming down the driveway. The garage opened with a touch of the newly-batteried remote, and I waited until the door rolled down behind me before getting out of the van. I knocked the *it's me* signal, used the key, and stepped into the kitchen.

"Hey," I called out

"Hey," she said from the living room.

I got a glass from the cupboard and put ice in it.

"Have you eaten?"

"Yup."

I selected a soda and poured it while Watson came into the kitchen and looked up at me.

"What's up, Buttercup?"

He rolled his eyes and twitched his head.

"'What's the deal, O'Neil?"

Again, he twitched.

"You want anything to drink, Mare?"

"I'm good."

"Come on, boy. Let's go see our girl."

I walked into the room and sat across from Mary in the big chair. She was wrapped in an afghan sitting in her spot on the couch with a soda in her hand, but she was not *good*.

When I raised my glass, she tipped back, a twinkle trying but failing to light in her troubled eyes. I turned to the right and raised my glass again but didn't receive a tip in return. Tasha did, however, pull her jacket open to show the gun and the ease with which she could draw it.

Through a torrent of thought and emotion, she noted Dax's calm demeanor and wondered if it was an accurate reflection of his feelings or an attempt to cover his concern. Either way, he appeared relaxed.

Sitting on the couch with Mary and watching Dax watch her, Tasha was again amazed at how the ordinary events of the morning had led to her discovery . . .

~

"Sorry it's taken so long, Detective Williams, but I have the information you requested. Do you still need it?"

"Well . . . Yes," Tasha said, taking the folder and putting it in the drawer of her desk. "Did you find anything?"

"Oh yeah. Lots of people dying within a hundred miles. Vehicular accidents, drug overdoses, suicides, homicides, drownings, shootings, stabbings. A lot of variety."

"Thanks, Karen. It's appreciated."

"You're welcome, Detective."

"Officer Walker?"

"Yes?"

"Could you just call me Tasha? Please? We've known each other for two years now," she said, grinning.

Karen nodded and went back to work.

Tasha leaned back in her chair and took a sip of sweet tea, thinking about Dax. He was starting to mean something to her. She felt a friendship forming and a good one at that. She'd been heartened by Jeri's encouragement, knowing she didn't give herself away easily or let many people in. Her opinions were fair and honest, and Tasha valued them.

Taking care to balance her love of sweet drink, she got up and went to the water cooler to rinse and fill her cup.

"Dom. Anything new from Chica? We could use some new art," she said, looking at the picture on the wall.

Dominic was talking with a retired parole officer from Albany, or as she liked to call it, *All-bini.* He liked to come in and shoot the shit with the detectives.

"Yeah, she tagged the IGA over in Apalachicola. I got the pic on my phone. Hang on. Hey, you know Steve, right?"

"Of course. Been catching any?"

"It's none of your business."

Tasha saw him try to contain the smile that always gave him away. Steve was funny – and a damned good fisherman.

"Well, if it *was* my business, and I put my boat in the water the next day or two, would I have better luck in the Bay or the Pass?" she asked. It had been way too long since she'd gotten a line wet.

"The tripletail bite is pretty good at Indian Pass. Just run the floats and noodles. Trout and reds are there, too. Lots of flounder in St. Joe Bay. It's on fire!"

The last time Tasha was in the Bait & Tackle shop, she'd heard him say the same thing to a customer using a camp-fire lighter as a prop. He liked to work there on the weekends to avoid the hundreds of boating tourists, or *tourons,* who came to spook and pressured his fish.

Dominic handed his phone to Tasha with a colorful picture in the frame. "It's a good one, maybe her best."

Chica Sanguine had upped her game, getting more creative in style and substance. She wasn't a fan of law enforcement but was telling some truth. Got to respect that.

"Will you send me the pic? It's so good, it's bad."

"Sure. Hey, Steve? Show Tasha that video," Dom said, and turned to her. "He's been using a drone to spot redfish, and he found a huge school of about four or five hundred a couple weeks ago. Right?"

"Yep. I whacked 'em. Probably caught two hundred."

Fishermen, Tasha thought. They don't lie so much as exaggerate the hell out of the truth.

"That's a huge school of reds. What were you using? Did you bounce some Gulp on the bottom or use a spoon? Are they still out there?" she asked him, her fishing juices flowing, wanting to be on the water and on some fish.

"I ain't telling you nothing. Those are *my* fish. I've already named them." His eyes lit with laughter, and Tasha knew he'd give it up eventually.

"Dom, I'm thinking of arresting this man for failure to fork over fishing information, but I'm afraid he'll lawyer up. Would you mind cuffing him while I look for that rubber hose? You know, the one we used to beat that girl scout who wouldn't tell us where those mint-chip cookies were."

Steve smiled as Dominic reached for his handcuffs.

"I was using a white worm and a gold spoon. Susan had a Wally-World tied on, and she hooked up with a . . ."

Tasha watched the video as he spoke. The dog, and the expression on its face, reminded her of Dax's. When the drone turned, she became unsettled but didn't know why. She couldn't see the girl's face, except for the smile, but something gnawed at her. When the camera zoomed closer, that something bit her.

Maybe it was the similar body type or because she was so desperate to find her . . . but she soon realized the girl she was looking at couldn't be Mary. This girl looked happy.

Tasha thanked Steve and gave him back his phone, and then went to her desk to find the *Mary* notebook, the one started when she thought there'd be a missing persons case. She leafed through it until she found an interview she'd conducted with a neighbor, Yvette Sommers. Her dog had gone missing the night before Mary and her father did.

Miss Sommers told her how close Mary was to Watson, and how they'd play like puppies when they were younger. She said Watson had acted strange for a week before he left – barking and seeming agitated. Yvette was heartsore and blamed herself for his leaving, said she'd practically kicked him down the steps before locking him downstairs.

"No wonder he left. Although how he got up and out the window, I don't know," she'd said, showing her a picture of the two *puppies* taken a year ago.

Tasha had asked to keep it at the time and found it now stuck between the pages of the notebook.

They look like friends, she thought. Solid, caring, I go where you go, friends. She leafed through her notes for the number and called Yvette to see if the dog had come home. Tasha commiserated and promised to call if he turned up.

She picked up the picture and perused and pondered.

Watson looked just like Doug, and she considered the coincidental odds of two owners having the same breed of dog with a connection to Mary – Dax's by way of her initial interest in his van and the reason for it.

Mary looked sweet with her arm around him, smiling, and Watson smiled right back at her.

Tasha sat up straight in her chair.

She lowered the Power-Pole and cast up shallow. A redfish tailed, and she swore because she'd thrown the orange popping-cork into the water with an empty hook at the end of the line.

On purpose.

The redfish laughed and teased her, swimming back and forth. Tasha automatically reached for the rod with the gold spoon before she stopped and stared at the red.

"Smartass. I'll be all over you, next time."

She pulled sharply at the popping-cork and continued to pretend to fish, the house visible through the trees. Tasha wasn't sure what she expected to see, especially with the sun low in the sky, and began to re-think what she'd been thinking a few hours ago at her desk.

Could Doug be Watson? Could Watson be with Mary? Could Dax have Mary?

Dax being involved in Mary's disappearance was only a fleeting thought weeks ago, dismissed almost immediately after she first spoke to him at Scallop Cove. She didn't really believe Dax had Mary or that Doug was Watson and wouldn't even be here except for that smile in the picture. The same smile she'd seen Doug give Dax.

But dogs didn't smile, did they?

Could Doug be Watson?

It felt like such a silly supposition, and it was why she'd rather peek through the trees than knock on the door.

The redfish and some of his friends pointed and stuck their tails up at her, making fun and having a good-old time. Right in front of the boat!

That's it. Tasha reeled in the popping-cork lickety-split and threw the gold spoon to the left of the cocky reds, beginning a slow to medium retrieve.

Eeny, meeny, miny - moe!

"Gotcha."

She heard someone telling someone else they'd be out in a minute. Tasha looked up from fighting her fish just in time to see the door close and Doug heading toward the back of the yard looking for a place to pee.

"Damn it," she whispered, fish on and pissed off. She'd have to reel in quickly without working him, increasing the risk the red would break . . . free.

"Damn, damn, damn."

She'd wanted to look that smart-aleck fish in the eye before letting him go. Now, he was running back to his fish friends and laughing at her. Again.

"Gosh darn it. I had him."

Tasha pulled in the spoon and quickly stowed the rod, raised the anchor-stick, engaged the trolling motor, and moved toward the wood-lined backyard. She let the boat drift closer then quietly slipped over the side and waded to shore, tying a rope around the base of a small tree.

She crept to the edge of the yard, keeping her eye on house and dog, and froze with the snap of a small branch. The dog turned his attention from the setting sun to her.

"Hey, Doug."

He cocked his head but didn't move.

"Watson," she said, her heart jumping when he wagged his tail. "Come 'eer, boy. Come on, cutie pie."

The dog rolled his eyes and stopped wagging his tail. Tasha thought he looked offended which made her chuckle. She tried again.

"I'm sorry, Watson. Would you come here, please? I'd like to scratch behind your ears if you wouldn't mind."

He smiled and walked over with what Tasha would later claim was eager anticipation.

chapter sixteen

Tasha stared at me, her eyes a kaleidoscope of emotion with confusion, anger, and relief distinct yet intertwined, all seen through the prism of her glare. There was also a look of disappointment that hit me like a hammer to the chest. I'd hurt her by not telling her.

She didn't say anything and hadn't pulled her gun, so I took a long sip of soda and started to rock in the chair.

"You okay, Mare?"

"So far, so good. You?" she said with eyes wide-open, asking for the truth.

"I'm right as rain."

I glanced at Tasha who was still processing, still not pointing her gun at me, and then back to Mary who looked at me quizzically.

"What does that mean, exactly? Right as rain."

"It means . . . Well, heck. I don't know. Why is the rain right? Why can't it be wrong? Or left?" I said, trying to coax a smile out of her. She gave a half-grin, instead.

"How long has she been here?"

"About twenty minutes."

I rocked in calm reflection while Tasha sat mulling. "Out of curiosity, how did she get into the house?"

"Watson," Mary said and glanced his way.

Watson avoided eye contact, looking at the floor, the wall, the ceiling, anywhere but at me or Mary.

"He stuck his nose through the side of his door but wouldn't come in."

"Is that true, Watson?"

When he kept gazing about, I asked if he was still upset I'd called him Doug. He peered over and rolled his eyes. I grinned and looked back to Mary.

"And?"

Mary was sheepish, not at all wanting to implicate herself just yet.

"Well, she was on the other side of the door, squatting and scratching him. You know how he gets when he's being scratched up," she said and started to squirm, knowing she hadn't answered all of the question he'd asked.

"And you know this, how?"

"Uh . . ."

"Did you investigate this suspicious nose activity by following protocol and checking the security camera from the safety of your locked room?" I asked, watching her struggle and knowing exactly what had happened.

This should be fun.

"No, I . . ." she said, trying to look away.

"Did you channel your inner Ninja and kneel by his nose and peek stealthily into his eyes?"

"Dax, no. I, uh . . ."

"Mare, you didn't just open the door and look, did you?" I was barely able to contain the smile ready to burst through my mock expression of disbelief.

"I . . . respectfully decline to respond."

I cracked up, and Mary started laughing. Watson smiled and came over to join the fun when I patted my leg.

Tasha watched the exchange with a *sincere* expression of disbelief on her face, still adjusting to the confusion of feelings that began the moment Mary opened the door. This outcome had been completely unexpected.

Her eyes softened at seeing the affection they had for each other, but Tasha was still on guard, still ready to put a bullet through Dax's head if need be. She looked at Mary and then Dax, wanting an explanation

"I know. There's a lot to explain. First, thank you for not just taking her away," I said, my eyes growing damp at the thought of coming home and finding her gone.

"Second. Would it be alright if I got you something to drink? Some water or a soda? We're going to be talking a lot in the next hour or so, I think."

Tasha nodded her head, needing answers before she took Mary into protective custody or not, arrested Dax or not. Decided to believe him. Or not.

"You still have some of the good stuff?" she asked.

I smiled. "One A&W, coming up."

Mary lifted her glass. "Me, too."

Tasha stopped me when I turned toward the kitchen. "Dax?"

"Yes?"

"I don't understand what's going on here, but Mary's safety is my primary concern. And I'm going to protect her. If you come out of the kitchen with anything other than rootbeer, I'll drop you in a heartbeat. I won't like it, but I'll do it all the same. No one is going to hurt her, anymore."

"I feel the same way, Tasha. In fact, I said just about the same thing in this very room once. But just for clarity's sake so there's no misunderstanding, when you say anything other than rootbeer . . . does that mean I can't have a Mountain Dew instead?"

Both Tasha and Mary smiled, and I took it as a good sign. Still, she hadn't said it was okay.

I better stick with rootbeer.

Despite the circumstance, the atmosphere was light and tension free as we drank our 'beer' in relative silence. I thought about how to begin and where to start, which would be tricky because of my uncertainty of what truth to use and how much of it to tell.

All depended on what the police could prove, not what they thought or thought they knew. Getting that kind of information, especially from someone as adept as Tasha, would be a challenge if not outright impossible. I started by trying to guide the conversation.

"Tasha, I think it might be a good idea if we . . ."

"Dax, listen," she said, putting the mug on the coaster and looking at me with solemn eyes.

"I'm going to ask Mary a few questions. Normally, I'd take both of you to the station and talk to you separately in different rooms, and Dax, if you interfere with her answers in any way, that's what I'll do."

She could have just called for back-up and removed Mary from the house, taking action if he tried to stop her. But she didn't think Dax would be the problem.

Mary would. Tasha didn't think she'd leave with her, voluntarily or otherwise.

"The reason I'm willing to talk here instead of the station, at least for the moment, is because . . . well, it's because there's something between the two of you that seems genuine. I'm also willing to suspend my suspicions for a short time if you'll let me do what I have to do. Will you respect that and give me a few minutes?"

I nodded as she took the gun from its sleeve, flipped the safety, and held it on her lap, finger by the trigger.

"Now, Dax. I like you. I want to trust you; I do. And if you'll just sit there and not make any sudden moves, I won't have to shoot you. Please tell me you understand the gravity of the situation we find ourselves in."

Tasha's eyes were serious business and I nodded, liking the hell out of her right now.

"I know exactly what you're doing and why. And let me say you are managing this moment correctly. Mare? Do you appreciate the way Detective Williams is trying to work with us and protect you at the same time? How she's hoping for the best but prepared for the worst?"

"I do. But I don't like her pointing the gun at you."

"I know, but she's right to do so, and she won't shoot unless she has to. I believe that. You can, too."

"Alright, but if she *does* shoot you I'm taking the Stevie Ray Stratocaster, just so you know," she said, smiling and winking at me.

Tasha was astonished at the depth of their relationship, and the contrast of the Mary she'd been afraid for and the one smiling and having fun with Dax. Momentarily taken aback, she wondered about her seeming transformation from hopelessness to happiness.

"Mary, I know I asked you this earlier, but now that I have a gun on Dax, you can tell me the truth. Were you kidnapped and brought here?"

"Nope."

"Are you here against your will?"

"Nope."

"Has Dax hurt you in any way?"

"Absolutely not. Dax saved me. In every way."

Tasha leaned back against the soft arm of the couch and let her words resonate. If they were true it would be like a miracle, and her heart felt the first stirrings of elation. But her optimism was tempered by realism.

"Mary, have you heard of something called Stockholm syndrome? It's when a person is held over a period of time and comes to . . ."

". . . have feelings or affection for their captor," Mary said, her twinkle burning bright as she looked at me..

"Is that it, Dax? Have you Stockholmed me? Is that why I'm putting Swedish meatballs in your spaghetti sauce?"

That's my girl. Quick of wit and mind.

"Honey, I appreciate your humor, really. It's one of my favorite things about you. But Detective Williams needs a serious answer to her question."

"That explains why I'm playing so many ABBA songs."

"Mary," I said, a little firmer than usual.

She nodded.

"Yes, Detective Williams, I've heard of it, and, no, I am not a victim of it. I come by my feelings for Dax legitimately. They were earned."

Tasha searched Mary for fear, conflict, nervousness, or deceit. Anything to indicate she was being forced to say it under threat of punishment if not spoken convincingly.

What she saw instead was sincerity and unabashed affection, her love for Dax fierce and tender, deep and unwavering. She could also see how the love Mary received nourished and strengthened her, something Tasha wouldn't have believed after seeing the devastated girl in the video.

She's not that little girl, anymore, she thought, and looked over to the recipient of Mary's devotion.

"Okay." She flipped on the safety and returned the gun to its sleeve. "Tell me. Tell me how she came to be here, why she left that night, and where is that . . . her father."

The way she'd asked about Mary's father gave me hope. Maybe there was a chance.

"I'll tell you if you tell me what's on the flash-drive you found, how many others have seen it, and if you'll consider what's really best for her before involving anyone else."

I became immediately afraid that our lives would be forever altered by my failure to just answer her questions. Tasha had been patient and measured in her actions up till now, but she could take Mary and go at any time. My heart sank when she reached for it . . . until I saw a coin in her hand instead of the gun.

"Call it," she said, and in an instant, we were back on the front porch. Her eyes lit up. The pretty ones; the ones I thought could be trouble. Could still be.

She smirked a little when I lost the toss.

"I guess you're not so good at this coin flipping thing, are you, Dax. It's me, two – you, zero, by the way. Not that I'm keeping score."

"Nooo., you're not competitive at all. But if you want, we can try it again. Mary, calculate the odds. Use the mathematical force to help restore honor upon this house."

Mary shook her head and grinned.

"There's a slight increase in favorable odds if certain conditions are met. Sometimes."

"Yeah? What are the conditions and how much of an increase? See how she's looking at me with those mocking eyes? Help me, girl."

The two of them looked at each other and laughed, enjoying the lighthearted banter.

"The odds of correctly calling a coin, rise from 50/50 to 51/49 if you call the side facing up on the toss. Of course, it assumes the tosser lets the tossee see the coin beforehand, and it doesn't factor in the height of the toss or the landing medium - hand, table, floor, carpet," Mary said, raising her hands to express the futility of knowing to a certainty something that was inherently incalculable.

132

"So, you're saying I can win? Thanks. I knew there was a reason I kept you around."

Tasha enjoyed the playfulness between them, wanting to be a part of it. But now, she needed to hear what had happened and why. And not from Dax.

"Dax, I'm going to ask something of you, something you might find difficult. But it's imperative if I'm to honor the tacit agreement I've made by virtue of the coin toss – consider what's best for Mary. I want you to leave us alone."

Mary and I communed in silence for a moment, no one but us, by and for ourselves.

"Are you alright with that?" I asked.

"Do you trust her?"

"As much as I can without knowing her very well. But I believe she cares about you and wants what's best. I'm willing to keep an open mind and give her a chance. Does that help?"

"The two of you know I'm still here, right?" Tasha said. She was fascinated by the bond they'd forged and the enjoyment they had with each other, even in as stressful a time as this.

"Oh yes, Tasha. We are aware of you. And I hope, you are aware of us, as well. Mary?"

"Okay, if you believe in her. But ... what if I can't talk about some things?" she asked, apprehension in her eyes.

"You talk about what you can, what you're comfortable with. It's your choice and only yours."

She looked at me for a few seconds and nodded.

"But Mare, whatever you decide to share, be honest and forthcoming. Can you do that?"

She moved her head up and down, slowly.

"Tasha, I'd like to freshen your beers and then go out and sit on the deck. Would that be alright with you?"

She nodded, and I went to the kitchen and poured fresh drinks into ice-cold mugs. After I'd returned and handed Tasha a glass, I began to set the other on the table, ignoring the coaster five inches away. A finger tapped on Mary's leg with a stern warning in the eyes of her tilted head.

"Love you, kid."

"Yup. You, too."

I picked at a Stevie Ray Vaughan tune that seemed appropriate to the moment as I sat on the deck and watched them through the window. Mary was crying, and I wished Tasha could just leave my little girl alone.

Seeing her suffer, even in the re-telling, made me want to bury him all over again. It wrenched my heart to watch, and I put down the guitar and peered up at the night sky. Watson came through his door and joined me.

"It's hard for you to watch, too, huh?"

Watson nodded. "Hard to listen to, as well. I had to get out of there."

I nodded and stopped.

Did he just say something? Did I just acknowledge what he'd said? He smiled as I cocked my head.

"Watson?"

He ignored my efforts to engage in conversation but came closer for some scratching, and I gave up and gave him what he wanted. I grinned when I found Mary's spot behind his ears and frowned when I saw her through the window.

While agitated about the pain Mary was in, I wasn't at all worried about what she'd tell Tasha. We'd planned for the possibility of being questioned by the police without knowing what they knew. When I told her to be *honest and forthcoming*, I was saying tell the truth, the entire truth. From the moment he touched her to the morning after I found her. After that, we only deviated in a few, minor ways – she'd been too afraid to leave my house and pleaded with me not to go to the police for fear of her father. She also hadn't seen or spoken to him or been back to her house since the night in the woods.

That's it. Just a few white lies. Nothing major.

Oh, and she didn't have any idea what happened to her father or where he could be, which, technically, had some truth to it. She didn't know where, precisely.

When I'd suggested turning myself in, she'd responded with anger and fear, saying she'd never forgive me if I did. Said it would be the same as leaving her.

134

She begged me not to.

Not with words but with her eyes, and it was nearly impossible to refuse her when she looked at me that way. Thank goodness, she didn't know it.

One issue was still problematic – the patrolman who'd seen the van. Could he identify Mary as the driver?

My original idea had been to ride a bike the eleven-plus miles to the hidden trail, walk to the house, take him and his truck, and leave the bike for someone else to find and enjoy. Adjusting the plan to accommodate her need to be there didn't significantly raise the risk. The patrolman seeing the van had been a fluke. Ten seconds either way, and he would have missed her altogether.

Maybe it had been a mistake to let Mary come with me, but I didn't know how to stop her, or if I even had the right. All he did, he did to her; it was her choice to make.

I looked through the window and witnessed something unexpected. Mary and Tasha were hugging and crying.

They wiped their faces and blew their noses using tissues Mary had stuck under the coffee table with the placemats, coasters, magazines, books, and newspapers, all neatly stacked with the remotes on top and pointed toward the television. She liked order.

And cleanliness, which might be her only flaw, but I overlooked it because her spaghetti sauce was so good.

Mary saw me looking and nodded. I rubbed up Watson, groaned as I stood up, and picked up the guitar.

"Let's go, boy. Once more unto the breech."

"Alright Dax, ask your questions. Then, I'm going to ask you some," Tasha said, after I'd played bartender and brought fresh drinks and a couple of jokes. When I sat in the big chair, she jumped from the couch.

"Wait."

"You know what they say about beer – you don't buy it, you only rent it. Or in this case, you only *root* it," I said, looking at blank faces looking back.

"You know, root it. Because we're drinking rootbeer instead of real beer."

"Oh, that's bad. Not funny bad, but awful bad. You should have quit with the *dog walks into a bar* joke."

Tasha turned and walked briskly down the hallway.

"Tasha's right, Dax. That was a clunker, big time. And I don't think Watson thought the dog one was very funny, either. Look at him. He's heading outside."

I told him I could change it to a cat instead, but he shook his head and left anyway.

"Man, I just about cleared the room. Am I losing it?"

"I don't know. Did you ever have it?" Mary asked with raised eyebrows and a wide-eyed expression on her face.

I frowned with some added sadness for effect, going for injured and confused. "You've been laughing at my jokes for months. What's up with that?"

"Well, you *have* been feeding me, and letting me stay here, and you did give up the big bedroom, so . . ."

Her brows remained raised even as her eyes laughed.

"You know I like it when you're a smartass, yes?"

"Yup."

After a second, I asked.

"How was it, Mare? Are you alright?"

"Yes. And it's surprising because I didn't think I would be. Or could be. People are going to know about it now, and that's going to be difficult for me, but I'm tougher than I was. And I won't be alone."

"Really? Who's gonna be with you?" I said, turning about some fair play with a wide-eye of my own.

She laughed and kicked my leg.

"Ahh . . . did you mean to kick me that hard?"

"Yup." Mary didn't like to think about a life without Dax, and the kick was a reminder of that fact.

I asked what she thought about Tasha.

"She's bright. Her questions were probing without seeming so, and she looked into me the way you do. It threw me at first, but I improvised, adapted and overcame."

Inwardly, I applauded her revision and use of an iconic movie quote, another great offering from Clint Eastwood. Water could be heard running in the bathroom sink.

"I believe she cares, really cares, about what happened to me, and I think she understood about . . . what I had to do. I didn't feel any judgement, and Dax, it meant a lot. You don't know how much . . ." She stopped and rubbed her foot against the leg she'd kicked. "Sorry. I know you know."

I nodded, and Mary got up and passed Tasha in the hall on her way to the bathroom.

There's a whole lot of peeing going on. Sounds like a country song, which reminded me of the blues song I was going to write – the lane of pain. *It's a sweet and just refrain.*

"Thanks for being so gentle with her, Tasha," I said when she sat down and reached for her drink.

"Dax, her story is horrific. And it's just amazing how strong and well-adjusted she's become in such a short space of time. I was so worried about her, and I'm so happy she's alive and well. It's . . . I am overwhelmed," she said, adding, "She loves you very much."

"I like her some, too," I said, asking quickly before Mary returned. "Do you believe her, Tasha? Do you believe she did what she did because she had to?" I didn't realize how hard I'd grasped the arm of the chair until she answered me.

"Absolutely."

I took a deep breath and nodded, leaning back into the chair before Mary swung it around as she walked by to sit in her spot on the couch. After looking back and forth between Tasha and me, she said, "So?"

Tasha told us about the flash-drive, how she'd found it, what was on it, how she'd felt about it, and what she'd done with it and why. When she said how Mary had seemed to look inside of her and how that made her feel, Mary and I looked at each other and Tasha stopped talking.

"What?"

"Tasha, do you believe in an intelligent being, a guiding force in the universe?"

"Well, I'm open to the possibility of God. But if He or She exists, I got a couple hundred-thousand questions starting with why He allows the innocent to suffer and the guilty go unpunished. Why do you ask?"

"Jesus," I said, and glanced at Mary who grinned and moved her head up and down.

"Do I take that to mean you believe in a deity?"

"Believe? Hell, no. But I've thought the same thing and shared it with Mary, almost word for word. The reason I asked is because sometimes things happen that make me seriously consider the reality of Him. Or Her."

Tasha tilted her head, asking for clarification.

"I saw those same pair of eyes, and they touched me, too. Profoundly and permanently. It's as if we were meant to see the same thing and share her pain. It's interesting and unnerving because I've become quite comfortable believing in my disbelief of a Lord moving in mysterious ways."

Tasha nodded, having a similar feeling. She asked Mary if she could have a moment alone with Dax.

"I'm going to ask a few questions, and then we'll talk about what comes next."

Mary lifted her eyebrows at me, and I gave a nod.

"It's all good in the 'hood. But if you wouldn't mind, could you and Watson go to your room instead of outside?"

"Why? Detective Williams has already found me."

"I know, but I'd feel better if you didn't go outside right now. I can't explain it. I guess I'm just a little unsettled about all this, and I want you to stay close where I can . . . I don't know. Would you indulge me, please?"

Mary nodded, and I saw a small tear peek around the corner of her eye. She knew what I was trying not to say. Now that we were known, I was frightened of losing her – to the police, to the world, even to the night. Despite all my preparations, the inner peace that served me so well had suddenly vanished, leaving me alone and afraid.

"Sure, I understand," she said and laid a hand on my shoulder, rubbing and patting a couple times before spinning the chair again on her way to get her guitar.

"Thanks."

"Welcome," she said and left with Watson in tow.

"She is a special young lady, Dax."

"Amen to that."

Tasha asked me to tell her everything. When I told her about stopping the video and seeing the desolation in Mary's eyes, I teared up.

"She broke my heart, Tash, and I haven't been the same since. I told her just what you did, no one was going to hurt her anymore, and I meant it. And bless that little girl; she believed me, and I've done what's needed doing to support her faith in me. Do you understand?"

"I do, Dax. She's lucky you found her. I can see how much you care. And not just for her emotional welfare, but you're teaching her how to survive, to be thoughtful and aware. She seems confident and looks capable of defending herself with purpose. Have you been training her?"

"Yes, and she's a fast learner. A tough little warrior with outside-the-box problem solving skills. She just about kicked my butt yesterday."

We listened to Mary play her guitar. Tasha's smile was full of delight, and my affection for her deepened.

"Damn. She's good."

"Yeah. I'd like to say she's just having a good day, but she plays like that all the time. No mistakes, no hesitations, no weaknesses. She plays circles around me and winks as she goes by, the little shit. I think she's a prodigy."

Her smile wavered for a moment, and a tear she thought I couldn't see formed.

"Tasha, I'm sorry. I wanted to tell you, especially after I saw how much you were torn up about Sara – and Mary. I came to believe you cared about her as a person, not just a statistic, and I wish I could have found a way. But she was safe with me. And I didn't know what you'd do."

She nodded, and I hoped she understood.

Mary came out of her room and put a hand on the back of the chair, ready to spin it as she walked by. I'd expected her to try it again and had a foot positioned to counter the clockwise rotation, but she anticipated my anticipation and spun me counterclockwise.

"Ha-ha." She sat down and looked back and forth. "So?"

I swiveled Tasha's way and asked the same thing.

"Yeah. What now?"

chapter seventeen

I put the last post in the hole, filled it partially with dirt, and tamped it down before pouring in the QUIKRETE. I'd give it four to six hours to set and dry before attaching the gate. In the meantime, I rolled a couple logs on the driveway and drove back to the house to shower.

Tasha had agreed to wait until I bought the gate and got the posts planted before coming to the station and start the process that would put Mary's father in jail. I would have preferred Mary, her story, and her location remained private, but Tasha said her father would have a legal right to take her unless she filed charges. Before I could say we'd just as soon wait until he came back, she'd said something I didn't have an answer for . . .

"Even if he doesn't come back for her, without the pressure of a warrant and letting the public know who and what he is, he could get close enough to some other girl to harm her. Maybe he already has. We can't let that happen."

'We don't have to worry about that, Tasha. He's been dead and buried for a while now,' is what I *wanted* to say. But, of course . . .

We all agreed there wasn't any reason for anyone to know how Mary escaped, and Tasha said it would only be a concern if her father had videos he could produce at trial. For the purposes of the police report, Tasha suggested Mary just say she'd freed herself and was afraid to call the police because he'd threatened to kill her if she told anyone.

She went over the probable charges – statutory rape, attempted murder, and a few more I didn't hear because I was watching Mary, surprised at how calm she was and how prepared she seemed to be. I hoped she was ready for this.

"I am."

"You am, what?" Tasha asked.

"I thought Dax said something."

"What? When? I didn't hear anything," she'd said.

~~

Mary sat waiting in the truck, her cheeks clean and rosy, her hair pulled back and tied in a ponytail. She looked as young as possible in the event Tasha had the patrolman take a good look at her. She hadn't asked Mary about the van and probably wouldn't, but she might want to tie up that loose end..

I would.

When we reached the logs, I rolled them to the side of the driveway, pulled the truck on through, and then rolled them back. It was a precautionary step. Our presence at the police station would come to the attention of the local news media, and, when they sent a crew in the *News at Six* decal covered van, their access to the house would be blocked.

Of course, the reporters could still walk down the driveway. But they'd find NO TRESPASSING signs posted, starting at the road all the way to the house. I'd put up some additional signs, as well - *WILL SHOOT FIRST, ASK QUESTIONS LATER*, and *I MAY GO TO JAIL, BUT YOU'LL BE DEAD*, and finally, *YOU'VE BEEN WARNED, DUMB ASS*.

If they triggered the 'black-eye', the electronic eye just inside the clearing close to the house, a shot gun blast would sound and small squibs would detonate in the trees.

If you don't know what a squib is, Google it.

For those who didn't leave and walked to the house anyway, a sensor would activate a highly pressurized spray of water, paint, and a touch of gasoline for smell. A fast back and forth rotation of the sprinklers would drench them quickly and hopefully, discourage their advance.

But, if they rang the doorbell . . .

Mary said I was crazy to stay up so late and rig the setup after Tasha left last night, but she helped me anyway, and we laughed at the thought of people sticky, stinking, and cursing. The security cameras would record it all, and we'd watch it on television, maybe make some popcorn.

We went by the Post Office so I could stop mail delivery for a while and then drove over to meet with Tasha and give our statements. I parked the truck and turned to Mary who was already looking at me.

"Feels strange driving around town in the daylight," she said, and I reached over to hold her hand. We shared a quiet moment, finding our calm and preparing ourselves.

I raised my eyebrow and she opened the door and said, "It's showtime."

~~

". . . birthday to Jewellllls. Happy birthday to you."

He watched her blow out the candles and squeal with delight when she got them all with one breath. She was thirteen, cute as a button, and nine days from being taken.

James had tried to quell the urge that first bubbled and then swelled, but it was now too strong to deny. He wanted what his brother had, absolute authority over his daughter – over Mary.

He'd thought about her a great deal, wanting to put his hands all over her and bring about that magnificent moan. Not since he was a boy had he heard anything so pure and persuasive, and he'd been reborn and energized by it. But Mary was gone - seized, sold, or dead.

So he'd find that indescribable euphoria with Jewels, cultivating her pleasure until she begged him to take her. That moment would be . . . transcendental.

James cared for his daughter, even loved her, but lust ruled his life. It always had, starting with his sister. The pain and agony his wife would suffer was inconsequential compared to the god-like power of taking what he wanted. Whatever or whomever it was.

He watched Jewels sit with her legs in the water beside the two preteens he'd arranged to have stolen with her. They were both pretty, with budding bodies, and would fetch a good price, ending up somewhere in the Middle East.

As the three girls stood up by the pool, James captured the image in his mind and looked them over in detail, from the tips of their toes to the tops of their heads, exploring every curve and crevice in between. One of them looked particularly enticing, but he might be biased . . .

He got up when he could and went inside to get a drink, nearly dropping it when he looked at the television.

Pictures of John and Mary were side by side as words scrolled along the bottom of the screen. A warrant had been issued for his brother, alleging physical and sexual abuse, the police asking people to call with any information leading to his apprehension. James moved closer, transfixed by the picture of his niece, hearing but not listening to the news.

" . . . her whereabouts for the last six months, since Christmas. Miss Stewart has been staying with a local resident who found her after she'd run away to escape the alleged abuse of her father. Her reason for not coming forward or contacting the police earlier is not known at this time. Police report the girl is healthy and seems to have been well cared for. No word about who or where . . ."

He almost reached for the screen, wanting to run his fingers along the underside of her jaw while his thumb brushed the smoothness of her face.

She's alive!

James could hardly contain himself. He'd have her after all, and the thought thrilled his soul. He knew she'd want him to come for her because of how she looked at him.

Not from the television screen – the eyes in that picture were of a schoolgirl full of innocence and wonder – and, while he envied his brother for taking that from her, it was how she'd look at him as he'd watch her that made it certain.

The eyes in those videos were submissive and obedient to the needs of her father, and she'd be the same with him after he reminded her of what she didn't think anyone knew – she wanted to be taken.

She needed to be.

He'd seen it in the way she moved her body, and how willingly she'd give in to her desire. James closed his eyes and thought about her writhing for and because of him.

"The music's getting ready to start, Daddy. You want to come dance with the birthday girl?"

~~

Kevin listened to the message and looked at his watch. He had plans for the night that would have to be canceled, and he wasn't happy about it. He could turn the job down and spend the night with Jackie, his friend with sometime benefits, but the thought vanished as soon as it entered his mind. You didn't refuse this man, not if you wanted to keep working for him. Certainly not if you wanted the bonus he offered. And Kevin most definitely wanted it.

He didn't know what more could be seen at Palmer's place, but he'd go take a look.

Maybe he'd stop by the Indian Pass raw bar on the way home, get some oysters and a few beers. Maybe bring some back for Jack. She wouldn't mind a late-night booty call.

She was good like that.

~~

Our time at the police station was less stressful than expected, due mostly to Tasha's care and Mary's calm. I'd been impressed by her composure and asked about it on the way home.

"It wasn't my fault, plain and simple. He drugged me, tied me down, raped me, and threatened to kill me. I did what I had to in order to survive, and I'm not going to blame myself for something I couldn't help. Not anymore."

"I'm glad to hear it, Mare. Your resolve is remarkable, especially given the circumstance. It's a great addition to your other notable attributes: courage, compassion, grace, honesty. Not to mention your intelligence, wit, and humor. Shall I go on?"

She got embarrassed and used her humor to deflect the self-consciousness brought on by the praise I had given.

"What else you got?"

I smiled and regaled her with an enumeration of her many gifts and talents as the hue of her red face deepened. She looked at me with tender cheerfulness.

"Sounds like you like me some," she said with a grin.

"You're alright."

She punched me and laughed.

I glanced at the rearview. The pearl white SUV was still following us. Tasha had arranged for a case officer from

Child Protective Services to meet us at the station, saving us a five to six-hour round trip to Panama City. That trip had been the reason for planting posts and rolling logs onto the driveway – to prevent looky-loos and news-crews from knocking on the front door in our absence.

Miss Harris had agreed to come by and do an inspection of the house, and Mary's accommodations, to include in her report. Based on her recommendation, the Court would decide whether Mary stayed with me, granting temporary custody, or was placed with another family.

She commented on the posted signs along the driveway with a smile, agreeing with the message they sent – stay out, or else. Fortunately, I'd remembered to disable the *black-eye* security sprinkler before she saw the craziness I liked to call *playful protectionism*.

Mary and I invited her to stay for dinner, but she smiled and said there was a family at home waiting for one of their own. We thanked her for coming, and she said, "I'm not supposed to tell you my recommendation, but . . ."

~~

Tasha had called late last night after finding Mary and told her everything. Jeri heard the relief in her friend's voice when Tasha said not only was Mary okay, she was thriving, due mostly to Dax's care.

She'd felt her pain as Tasha talked about Sara, about how much it still hurt, wishing *she'd* had someone like Dax and wishing she could have been that someone. Jeri hadn't let her friend take more responsibility than was reasonable and asked Tasha to be fair to herself and find some peace.

"So, how did it go?" Jeri asked when Tasha called again at noon. She told her about Dax and Mary coming to the station and giving their statements.

"It sounds like Mary's going to be alright, Tash," she said, adding, "You, too."

Jeri laughed when Tasha told her about Watson and waved in the Deputy-Director when he stood at her door.

"Okay, girlfriend. It's back to the grindstone for me. Live long and prosper."

Robert Thompson held up his hand in a failed attempt to give a Vulcan greeting.

"I saw an episode of Star Trek last night and thought I'd give it a try after hearing you say, 'Live long and prosper.' But I can't quite get my fingers to move right,".

Jeri smiled. "There's a trick to it. My friend Tasha showed me. Oh, by the way, you wanted to know how her investigation was going . . ."

~~

The newly installed gate opened and closed as I pushed the button. The number of remote controls were beginning to get out of hand - gate, warning, alarm, garage door, simulated shotgun with squibs and security sprinklers. It occurred that I may have a problem, and the first step, as they say, is admitting it.

Hi. My name is Dax, and I'm a remotaholic.

But, I was a remotaholic with a sweet little girl making a pre-celebratory spaghetti dinner with all the fixins – garlic bread, mounds of grated parmesan and mozzarella, corn on the cob, a big salad, strawberry cheesecake, and plenty of milk and sweet tea.

If life wasn't all good, it certainly wasn't half bad.

~~

Three weeks after Tasha found us, Mary and I were still adjusting to leaving the house and being seen as opposed to staying home and being careful. Caution was a hard habit to break and, rather than abandon it, we repurposed it.

Fortunately, Mary's story hadn't attracted the attention of the national media. Still, two news-crews from Panama City hounded us for the first week or so, and both had breached the barrier of the gate – accomplished by walking past the posts.

Both crews triggered the simulated shotgun blast, and both were saturated with paint and gasoline. One intrepid individual even pressed on to the house, leaving a Mohave colored stain on the porch.

When she rang the doorbell, a recorded voice said, "Regret in t-minus five, four, three, two . . ."

It was television worth watching and Mary and I played the video over and over.

I'd sent copies to the station directors and their legal departments, threatening to send one to the State Attorney General and sue them for blatant disregard of private property rights and endangering the safety of the occupants of my house and their personnel.

Additionally, I said I feared for the life of myself and my charge, reminding them we lived in a *Stand Your Ground* state and that any attempt to approach my house would be construed as a home invasion – with all the protections and provisions that particular law provided.

The news directors hadn't taken me seriously, though.

So the next time it happened, I came around the side of the house with a shotgun, ordered two cameramen and a reporter to lie face down on the ground, and zip-tied their hands and feet. I then called the police and pressed charges when they arrived.

Tasha called early the next morning. The *Live at Five* station manager promised to cease and desist if I'd drop the charges. She chuckled as she told me how he'd first demanded and then pleaded with her captain to intervene. She said we had tons of support at the station house, most of them approving of my methods. And my madness.

"I'll drop them if he agrees to keep his person and employees one hundred feet from Mary, me,, my property, and my vehicles. He'll need to put it in writing, and have copies faxed or delivered to my attorney, the local state's attorney, your department, and the *News at Six* station manager, as well, so they'll know what's what. And Tasha?"

"Yeah?"

"He needs to do it, without exception or modification, before two this afternoon. Not a minute after, otherwise, I'll go to court and ask for a restraining order and probably get it, which won't sit well with his viewers or stockholders."

The agreement was received by Tasha's boss three minutes shy of the deadline. He called it *some funny shit.*

~~

I took her to see Mrs. Hunter for a visit, one that began with an emotional greeting. She'd started crying the moment she saw Mary and wrapped her arms around tight, unwilling to let her go. Mary crie, too, and they soon went inside the house while Watson and I went for a walk.

"They seem to have an affinity for one another," I said.

"If you mean a kinship, then yes. Mrs. Hunter is a good mentor and has encouraged Mary's passion for learning, especially in higher mathematics."

"I wonder if she'll want to go back to school? She's surpassed the educational level of most of her peers by now, but it could still be challenging, socially. Might be tough."

"You're right about that, but she may surprise you. Mary's capacity to overcome adversity has been a hallmark of her development for as long as I've known her. Well, for as long as I became aware that I noticed it. But her current state of readiness is, in no small part, due to you and your encouragement. You've done well."

"Thanks, I appreciate that. You've also done right by her, and I'm grateful for that."

"Thanks."

"Hey, Watson?"

"Uh-huh?"

"Don't you find it a little odd we seem to be talking to each other?"

"There are more things in heaven and earth, Dax, than are dreamt of in your philosophy," Watson said with a smile on his face.

I literally scratched my head.

"Listen, as long as I'm imagining we're talking, can I ask a couple of questions?"

"Sure."

"What's up with you guys sticking your nose in every crotch you come across? And why're y'all licking yourselves all the time?"

"What? Are you jealous?"

We drove over to Yvette Sommers' who was overjoyed to see them. She cried and told Watson how sorry she was for brutally kicking him down the stairs and locking him in the lower room. He told her he was fine, she'd only nudged him a little, but she didn't understand him and never would. He looked at Mary who nodded as he shook his head. Not many understood each other as well as they did, and both knew how lucky they were.

When it came time to leave, Watson stood by Mary's side, hoping Yvette understood the meaning. She nodded, kneeled, and gave him a hug.

"Will you come by for a visit from time to time?"

He gave her a nod but rolled his eyes when she said it was movie night on Thursday.

"You want to go visit?" I asked when I leaned over and opened the door to let her and Watson into the truck.

Mary looked at her house across the street and shook her head. "There's nothing for me there. Let's go home."

~~

Seeing Mary through Palmer's living room window had been worth every penny he'd paid Kevin. His heart jumped with joy, and he ached to get his hands on her.

But first, he needed to extract her from her guardian.

James knew he would protect her without hesitation. They obviously cared for each other, and it gave him an idea how to draw Mary out of the house and into the plastic-covered trunk of his car.

He leaned back in the chair, his hands in a steeple under his chin, and contemplated the obstacles he'd face. He could have someone else bring her to him, which would be less risky but not as satisfying. James wanted to see her eyes when he took her from the security of her new home to his place in the woods.

The cabin was isolated, sound-proofed, and secure. No one had ever escaped, and neither would she. It's where he and John had enjoyed many young girls over the years, and where he'd explore every inch of Mary's body and desire.

James' vacation plans were set.

His wife always looked forward to his time away alone, knowing he'd come back from his *fishing trip* relaxed and invigorated, ready to rekindle the fire of their passion. She thought something in the sun and salt air brought him home ravenous in his hunger for her.

There's something, alright, he thought.

The juxtaposition of a child's unwilling compliance and his wife's unrestrained enthusiasm was a sexual delicacy he savored after returning from his interludes at the cabin. Those caught and captive girls were an aphrodisiac, and his wife the happy recipient.

And soon, she would be again.

~~

Her case load was light, a brief respite from the non-stop cycle of humans behaving badly, and Tasha used the time to clean her desk, starting with the drawers.

After a few minutes, she picked up a folder containing information she'd asked Officer Walker to compile weeks ago – deaths within a hundred-miles of St. Vincent.

At the time, and brought on by bored curiosity, she'd been interested in any deaths in or around places Dax had played. But his involvement in them had never been a serious consideration – nor was Mary driving that van . . .

~

When they'd come in to give their statements, she asked patrolman Petersen to see if Mary and Dax would like a snack or something to drink while they waited for her to finish her phone call – which was a pretense so she could watch the interaction between them.

Tasha hadn't told him who they were but had an eerie feeling that Dax's smile to her wasn't so much a greeting as an acknowledgement of who Petersen was. After they'd left the station house, she asked the patrolman about them.

"I've seen Palmer play at Scallop Cove and up in Wewa. He's pretty darn good. Haven't seen the girl, though. She's a cute kid."

"Yeah. She is."

Afterward, she'd been asked to come over for dinner and music but hadn't wanted to intrude or add to the stress of unwanted visitors to their home – strangers or newsies or strange newsies. She'd laughed out loud the first time someone got 'sprinkled.'

When the public interest in them waned, Dax played the Mary card, saying her feelings would be hurt if she didn't at least come by to see how she was doing. Tasha didn't know if he'd sounded pitiful on purpose, but she did want to see them.

So, she had.

They'd laughed and played music, talked about some things and not about others. It was easy to be around them, their humor infectious and generous, loving and playful. They welcomed her with warmness, and her affections had deepened as they spent more and more time together.

Tasha looked at the folder in her hands and almost pitched it in the wastebasket. But the *trust but verify* part of her turned a cursory examination into a mini-investigation.

After a process of elimination, she made a list of twelve deaths by unnatural causes and ran them through the system. Five had criminal records for drugs, vehicular manslaughter, stalking, child abuse, and aggravated assault.

The drug dealer had been shot in the face, the stalker strangled with a garrote, the pedophile castrated and eviscerated, the man who beat his ex-wife stabbed with an icepick and shot, and the drunk who'd run over the school kids had himself been killed in a hit and run.

She thought the pedophile and drunk could have been killed by the same person given the specific manner of their deaths. Maybe they all were.

But it couldn't be Dax.

chapter eighteen

If you weren't there that night, you missed it.

Not the performance, you could find some of it on YouTube, but the feel of it, the atmosphere and electricity. The knowing you'd seen something special.

We played for three hours across a wide spectrum of musical genres, from rock to ballad, blues to country, even some bluegrass and a few jazz instrumentals. I thought word must have spread across town, because the size of the crowd spilled out and into the parking lot.

Mary played at the highest level of perfection and left me in the dust, while Tasha held her own for periods of time that would have been longer if she'd played or practiced more in the last five years.

I was in awe of them both and counted myself lucky to be a part of what would be a night I'd always remember. Mary was in her glory, loving to play and being loved for her playing. She was used to my praise, but the reaction of the crowd would surely have an impact on her. How could I keep her down on the farm, after she'd seen *Paree?*

The people clapped and chanted her name for minutes after we'd finished, and she looked at me with a light shining in her eyes, tears forming and falling down her cheeks, laughing and crying at the same time. She looked so happy.

My eyes were wet as I nodded. If you could have seen the expression on her face, you would have teared up too.

Tasha reached over and gave Mary a hug, patting her shoulder with one hand and holding the bass with the other. Mary leaned into her and slid an arm around Tasha's waist, giving a hug in return.

It was a sweet and beautiful moment.

We started to break down the equipment, ready to load the van and leave the warm embrace of the appreciative Scallop Cove congregation. I nodded when Mary said she was heading to the bathroom and, a minute later, Tasha said the same.

"Okay, I got this. See y'all in a bit."

Tasha was surprised by the number of people who praised her performance along the way. She thanked them, flattered and embarrassed, but thought her bandmates more worthy of appreciation.

Dax's presentation was visceral and full of passion, and Mary's playing and singing came from the heart, inviting the audience to feel what she felt and love the music the way she did. They set a high bar, and Tasha thought she'd have to bone up to keep up.

She eventually reached her destination and saw Mary speaking to someone unfamiliar to her.

"Listen. She doesn't want to go home with you. Is that correct?" Mary said, asking the woman behind her without taking her eyes off the man in front of her.

"No. I mean yes, I don't want to go with him. I want him to leave me alone," she answered, her voice trembling.

"There you go. No misunderstanding about what she wants, right?" Mary was calm, assessing the situation moment by moment without moving her head.

"Who the hell do you think you are? Get the f . . ."

Tasha moved forward when he reached for her but then stopped and stared.

In a few seconds, Mary blocked his arm, drove the heel of her palm into his nose, grabbed his shirt and buried her knee in his crotch, then stepped back and cracked the side of his lowered head with an elbow thrown like a fist.

She stood over him in a relaxed and ready stance.

"Are we done here, then? If not . . ."

The man put up a bloody hand, the other between his legs holding on like it would make the pain go away.

Mary asked the woman if she needed a ride home.

"No. Thanks. I . . . thanks," she said, and then pushed through the crowd that had formed around the prone figure groaning on the floor.

Mary walked through the door, and Tasha followed her into the bathroom.

"Mary? Are you alright?" Tasha saw her hands shaking, as well as the smile she received.

"Yes. That was interesting and scary. Did you see it?" Mary took a couple of deep, controlled breaths.

"I only saw the last part. From right before he reached for you."

Mary nodded, feeling better, calmer, less shaky.

"He had his hands on her and wouldn't let her go into the bathroom. She looked scared, so I got in between them and backed her up."

Tasha was impressed with her courage and told her so.

"You helped that woman. A lot of people would have stayed out of it. It says something about your character. Something good."

"Thanks."

Tasha looked at Mary with fresh eyes. Dax called her little, sometimes - *little shit, little girl* - but she was lithe, athletic, and able-bodied. She comported herself well beyond her years and could easily be mistaken for a young college woman. You'd have to catch her in an unguarded moment to see the truth of her youth.

"Were you afraid you'd get hurt? You said it was scary."

Mary shook her head.

"You know, maybe I should've been, but it didn't cross my mind when I got between them. I was scared I wouldn't be able to protect her, and that worried me," she said, looking away a moment before continuing.

"And then I was scared I'd hurt him too much, and *that* worried me."

"Why?"

Mary told her the truth.

"Because I wasn't worried if I hurt him, because he wasn't going to touch her again."

Tasha nodded and touched her arm. She understood what Mary meant. If the choice was between hurting that man or his harming that woman, that man was going down.

"What did you mean when you said it was interesting?" Tasha asked, and Mary broke into a smile.

"The things Dax has taught me are part of me now. I acted instinctively but carefully. I correctly assessed the situation, looking for threat or advantage. I guess that's why I wasn't afraid for myself, because there was a job to do that I could do. Don't you find that interesting?"

Tasha nodded and smiled with her.

"Will you tell Dax what happened – if the story hasn't already spread through the Cove?"

"Probably. But please, let me do the telling. I want to process it all first. Believe me, there'll be a question and answer period afterwards," she said and laughed. Tasha joined in and felt closer to Mary. And Dax, through her.

They slowly worked their way back to the stage as people expressed their appreciation for giving them a night they would long remember.

~~

She listened to the squeak of the big chair rocking and the snore of the big dog sleeping. Mary rolled over and looked at Watson lying on the carpeted floor. He was running in his dream, and maybe she'd find out why in a bit.

Based on her interpretation of the chair's Morse code, she surmised it had to do with an upcoming job, the playing for sure but, more probably – the slaying.

Someone, somewhere, had done somebody wrong.

Mary believed in the rightness of Dax's decision to mete out justice, and the confrontation at Scallop Cove tonight reinforced that belief. She felt empowered and uplifted, not because she knocked the man to the floor, but because she'd helped that woman and kept her from harm.

Dax trained her to be capable, to defend herself, but it was something inside that compelled her to intervene. To step up and step into the conflict rather than run from it.

Like she'd done with her father.

When bound to her bed and in the depth of her despair, she had chosen to fight for her freedom. To accomplish it, she'd flipped a switch in her head, one later understood as a break from herself, a dissociative state of mind that allowed her to think of the man who touched and raped her as a stranger, instead of the dad who raised her.

It was the only way she could do what she'd done.

Mary still felt a burning hatred for that man and never had a moment's regret for his being in the ground, a rotting corpse who only received half of what he deserved.

When the chair stop squeaking, she knew somebody, somewhere, at some time, would reap what they'd sown.

Dax would see to it.

~~

No matter how hard he tried, Watson couldn't catch it. Not by running faster or slower, not by creeping up on or lunging at it. He tried once more, jumping and thinking he'd catch it off-guard.

"So, this is what you're running after," Mary said, smiling and shaking her head. "This is what you've been chasing in your sleep?"

"It's right there. I can get it. I know I can," he told her, looking at his tail.

"How about a little air time?" she said, rising with ease. "Come on up, and I'll chase it with you."

~~

In the weeks since our debut at the Cove, we'd been asked to play eight different events: two festivals, two bars, three beach parties, and one wedding.

We'd played all but one bar, because their liquor license didn't allow minors, and only the one festival. Afterward, Mary said she preferred the intimacy of the bars and parties instead of wide-open festivals, and, because she was the one everyone wanted to see, it was her decision.

Or so I told her.

There'd been too many people wanting her attention at the festival, too many for me to keep an eye on. It made me nervous. Smaller venues were easier to manage.

Tasha joined us at the wedding, the festival, and of course, the beach parties. She shared Mary's love of sand, surf, and sun, and being in, under, and on the water. She'd taken her out on her boat a few times, and they'd fish or lay on the deck to catch some rays. Mary got a bad sunburn early on from being indoors so many months, but now had a dark, golden tan.

I'd been granted temporary custody of her. The judge told us the conditions of the order were subject to change depending on the father's appearance or standing after any legal proceeding.

In other words, she was mine – with all it entailed, as I found out one day at the beach when she was talking to a boy who was twenty if he was a day. He was flirting with her, encroaching into her personal space, and she was laughing and letting him.

I suddenly noticed she wasn't a little girl but a young woman. A beautiful young woman with a young woman's body, and I wondered why she'd worn such a small bathing suit, and how come he looked at her chest when she leaned down to smack a yellowfly on her knee, and what the hell he'd said that had been so damned funny . . .

I called her over, trying to get a handle on new and disconcerting emotions. Tasha waved and gave me a smile I'd later comprehend.

"What's up?" Mary asked.

"Yeah."

"What?"

"Yeah. That's what *I* want to know. What's up?"

Her confusion was genuine but didn't stop my growing anxiety as my face flushed, and my eyes conveyed whatever I was feeling.

"What? Why are you looking at me like that?" she asked, a little irritation creeping into her voice which caused more of my own to peer at her from my stare.

"What are you doing with that boy? Why are you letting him stand so close to you? And how come your wearing such a . . ."

"Hey, guys. What's up?" Tasha said as she walked over.

158

I glared at her, then at Mary.

"That's what I'm trying to find out," I said with a tone fueled by an ire I neither understood nor could suppress.

Both girls had a reaction to the sharp edge in my voice – Tasha chuckled, and Mary got pissed.

"Don't use that tone with me, Dax. I don't like it," she said with one of her own that meant business..

"I'm sorry, Mare. I shouldn't have done that. But I want you to stay away from that boy. He's too old, and you're too young, and . . ."

"Dax? I'm going to take her for a little walk. Is that okay with you, Mary?"

Mary nodded, her anger vanishing as quickly as it appeared, replaced by confusion and sadness.

My irritation dissipated the moment I saw her angst. As they walked away, I felt awful and hoped I hadn't done any damage. Why had I been so bothered? She could take care of herself and put him down if she needed to. So, what was wrong with her talking and laughing with that boy?

That horny, twenty-something, trying to get into her pants *son of a bitch* . . .

My brain informed me a message had just arrived from the processing department. It was short and sweet.

'Welcome to parenthood.'

My intellectual understanding of having custody meant I was her guardian, and, until a few seconds ago, that was all I thought or thought I knew. But the emotional reality sucker-punched me in the stomach.

I have a daughter.

A strong, intelligent, exceptionally talented daughter. And the pride I felt was quickly tempered by the realization of why I'd had such a vexing reaction to her and that boy.

She was also beautiful, graceful, and athletic, with a dazzling smile and long wavy hair – plus a variety of other attributes guaranteeing any horny-something *son of a bitch* would now be hanging around my no longer little, little girl.

Now I ask you, did I overreact to that boy standing so close to my daughter? I think not.

And what the hell had been so damned funny?

In all the times I'd been teaching her to protect herself from harm, I hadn't once thought about her interaction with boys. I didn't even consider the possibility of her becoming sexually active, especially after what had happened to her. And that was understandable, because I didn't know what the future would be or how long we'd be together.

But now it might be a conversation we'd have someday, and I wasn't ready for that.

Maybe I'll just lock her up in her room till she turns thirty, I thought, and then grimaced. Bad, bad adage in this case.

The girls were joking around as they walked my way. Tasha nodded at me and I returned it, knowing I'd thank her later. She was special in her own right, and I valued her friendship more and more.

Mary ran the last thirty feet, kicking up sand on the surf and smiling all the way. I stood and she jumped, expecting me to catch her, which I did . . . and then immediately fell backwards into the water.

When we came up for air, her eyes were shining.

"What was that about?" I asked.

"Congratulations. It's a girl."

~~

"No, Daddy," she said, as his hand covered her mouth.

"Stop it now, or it'll hurt. It'll hurt, and you'll wish it didn't. Just relax." He pushed himself between her legs, and she could see the pleasure he took in taking her.

Tasha bit down hard, drawing blood, and glared at him. He pulled his hand away and looked at her.

"I said *no,* damn it."

He couldn't believe his ears. She loved it when he touched her, always had, and today he was giving her the gift of womanhood as a birthday present.

She'd been excited last night talking about it, agreeing it was special, something they would share only with each other and no one else. He'd smiled when she asked how anything could feel better than what they'd been doing.

Tasha had gotten nervous after he told her it might hurt the first couple times, saying she liked the way he touched her now – and the squirmy feelings that followed.

"I know, hon. Me too. But I'll be real gentle. You'll see. We'll do what we always do and just add something new. Hey, it rhymes. And the squirmies you'll feel after that will be ten times better. How 'bout it?"

She'd eagerly said yes, which was why he looked at her now in disbelief. He tried priming the pump, but she yelled.

"Stop it, Daddy! I mean it. I don't want this. It's wrong, and it's evil, and I'll kill you if you ever touch me again. Now get the fuck off me!"

Tasha sat bolt upright from her dream and felt the tears on her face, but not the shame that usually accompanied them. Instead, a new feeling sprang up and washed over her, one of release and freedom. She had never challenged her father before, never been able to stop him until tonight, and every part of her sang out in joyous harmony of mind, body, and spirit as the heavy shackle finally fell away.

She began to sob . . . for the little girl in her dreams, the one she was leaving behind. She loved that girl but couldn't visit her anymore. Tasha had finally broken free.

And she was never going back.

~~

I've always enjoyed driving – here, there, or anywhere. It gave me time to think.

I was heading to Destin, ostensibly to play a gig at the Hog's Breath Saloon, the bar where I'd found Mr. Dobson sitting and drinking, the place I'd played three nearly perfect songs, which had been the most memorable night of my musical life until the night at the Cove with Tasha and Mary – the same night Elisabeth Dobson asked for my help.

While Mary had been protecting that woman by the bathroom, a waitress handed me a phone. Elisabeth first thanked me for visiting her in the hospital, then apologized for intruding, telling me she'd seen my picture on television. A news reporter said I occasionally played guitar at Scallop Cove on Cape San Blas.

Thanks a lot, Channel Thirteen. People certainly had a first amendment right to know that. What passed for news these days was sad and troubling.

Elisabeth didn't explicitly ask for my help, but I heard the pleading in her voice as she told me about her friend, her best friend, and how desperate she'd become and why.

Nothing incriminating was expressed. She was just telling *a friend* about another friend's problems, looking for commiseration by extension, asking me to listen and care. Hoping I would.

"I'm sorry to hear that, Miss Dobson. Sounds like she's having a time of it. How about you? Been doing alright?"

She was good now, and the lightness in her voice said it all. I asked a few questions before saying goodbye, and then began to consider her friend's problem.

I remembered the Hog's Breath manager asking me to come play sometime, and after a quick call, I had a legitimate reason to be in the city. Because it was a liquor bar, Mary wouldn't be able to play, so I'd have some truth on my side when I told her why she couldn't come.

"What are you thinking about?" Mary asked, sitting next to me in the van on my way to Destin.

"About you're not coming on this trip because you couldn't play in the bar." I smiled and looked over.

"And how happy you are that I came anyway, right?"

She smiled back.

"I hadn't gotten that far yet, but, yes. I am."

And I was.

Since being baptized in the waters of the Gulf of Mexico as parent and child, we'd been open and playful in our new familial roles.

For fun, I'd declared a nine o'clock bedtime one night, flexing my parental muscles, showing her who was boss. She threw a fit, said I was being mean, that she was a big girl and it wasn't fair. Then she stomped her feet all the way to her room and slammed the door.

Parent 1, Child 0.

"I'm thirsty. Can I have a glass of water? Pleeeease. I'm dying of thirst. I need water. Pleeeeeease. I'm thirsty."

That went on for 30 minutes.

Parent 1, Child 1.

Later I thanked her for not throwing in an *I hate you* as she'd stomped off. She said it would lose its power after the first time and was waiting for the right moment to use it – like after I caught her with a boy when she was supposed to be staying overnight at a friend's house.

Mary said the look on my face was hilarious, and she laughed so hard she peed a little. I gave her props, as the kids say, commended her use of an *imagined* sore spot to help sell it, said it was one of the things I liked so much about her, and then grounded her until she was seventy-eight.

"Sure you'll be okay at the hotel? I'll be late getting in."

"Yup. I've got on-line tests to study for, college courses to look over, my guitar to play and Watson to keep me company," Mary said, glancing back at her sleeping friend.

I asked if she might want to go back to school in the fall, saying she'd probably test out as a senior. She said probably not, preferring to remain schooled at home.

"Then again, I'll bet those 12th grade boys are all kinds of cute. Don't you think?"

This was going to be a thing now, and she'd have her fun like I did with her coasters. But it wasn't quite the same – because that coaster wouldn't try to feel me up one day. Of course, I couldn't let on that it bothered me as much as it did for the obvious reason.

She'd push that button all - the - time.

~~

Tasha couldn't remember when she'd slept so late and awakened so refreshed. She'd been smiling all morning thinking about her dream, what it meant, and what it could mean. Ever the investigator, she asked herself the pertinent question. What made last night's defiance possible?

Dax and Mary.

The tempest of her troubled spirit had calmed since she'd told Dax about Sara. She couldn't explain it, but his tenderness that night had lightened her heavy heart.

And Mary's struggle to survive had touched her deeply. She'd saved herself from an evil man, and Dax had saved her from the emotional repercussions.

The love and respect they shared was a special thing, and Tasha had been invited to become part of it, to laugh with them, to play and grow with them.

And she'd been strengthened by it.

Maybe she'd tell them her story one day. She'd like to thank them for being who they were and tell them what they meant to her. Perhaps when they got back from Destin.

chapter nineteen

Mary raised an eyebrow when I told her I was leaving for the gig. She looked over to the window and back at me, at her watch, back to me, over to Watson, and then back . . .

"Yeah, I know. It's still light outside, and it's a few hours before I play."

"A few?" she said, trying to look into me before I knelt on the floor to rub up Watson.

"Dax?"

"Now Mare, if you want to know why I'm leaving so early, just ask."

"Why are you leaving so early?"

I looked up and grinned. Watson nudged my hand to keep rubbing and talk later.

"Have I told you I like you, lately?"

"No, you haven't."

"I like you lately," I said and gave her a pretty good wide-eyed expression of affection.

"That's sweet. I like you lately, too. Why are you leaving so early?" she asked with a wide-eye of her own.

Hers was much better than mine. I gave Watson a final scratch and pat and then stood up and told her.

"A friend of mine needs a favor for a friend of hers."

"What kind of favor?"

"My friend's friend is worried about her daughter's daughter. I'm going to see if she's okay, or if she needs help."

"Why can't she do it? Your friend's friend."

"It's a long way to Tipperary."

She raised a brow.

"It's an old British song. Sorry. It's a long drive for Naomi, and her daughter wouldn't talk to her even if she came. She's tried," I said.

"What kind of help might she need?"

"She thinks her daughter's living conditions aren't ideal for raising a child. If true, something would have to be done about that."

Mary nodded and gave my words some thought. "So, you're doing an inspection of current living conditions to ascertain whether a change in circumstance is warranted?"

Like me, her analytical language tends toward brevity.

"Yes. That's a concise iteration of the situation," I said, wondering if she knew or wanted to know what I was really up to. How would I respond if she did?

"Is there any question I might ask about this . . . situation, that you'd *respectfully decline* to answer?"

A seriousness in her voice made me carefully consider my response. "Do you agree I have the right to decline?"

She nodded.

"And will you accept it if I was inclined to decline?"

She liked having fun with words and gave me a grin. "Of course."

"Then, no. No question about this situation will be answered thusly. If it's important enough for you to know; it's important for me to tell you."

"Okay. Just checking. And Dax - thusly? What are you, a hundred? Who uses that word? " she said, punching my arm and then running away when I reached for her. Watson kept me from chasing her by pulling on my pant leg.

"Come back here, you little . . . Thusly, I say. Obey me," I commanded with my *father of creation* voice.

~~

You want to know the hardest thing about killing, about taking the lives of other people, at least for me?

Transportation.

Do I use my own vehicle or a rental? Each has an up and down side along with a corresponding risk and reward. I'd only stolen one vehicle, which added another level of risk but was necessary to bring some symmetrical justice to some murdered school kids.

Also, getting to and from my target was a challenge.

166

First - I needed to keep the vehicle and license number from being seen or recorded. Which wasn't easy given that everyone had a phone these days and used it like a camera.

Second - I had to leave the vehicle far enough away to avoid detection, but close enough to avoid having to take a shuttle to get where I was going.

I'd had to walk, run, or ride a bike for miles in order to find and kill my guy or girl. Sure, I'm more fit because of it, but I'd rather get in quick, get it done, and get some cheesecake instead of having miles to go before I eat.

Maybe it's not transportation so much as parking?

Miss Dobson told me her friend's daughter lived with a dealer who'd gotten her into drugs. Naomi thought he beat her sometimes, but her daughter always denied it, said she loved him, and told her mother to stop interfering.

But that wasn't why Elisabeth had called me.

Every other week, Naomi would drive to Destin, pick up her granddaughter and take her to Tallahassee for the weekend, and then bring her back on Sunday night or take her to school Monday morning.

The little girl was the delight of her grandmother and every trip and visit an enjoyable time for them both. Except for the last two when the girl was withdrawn and nervous and all attempts to find out why were met with silence.

Naomi thought the boyfriend might be hurting her but was told she couldn't see her granddaughter anymore when she brought it up to her daughter. She'd gone to the police about it, but the girl told them it wasn't true and she was fine. Naomi didn't believe it and was afraid for her.

So, I'd come to see if her suspicion was justified or just speculation. Me and my shadows.

Elisabeth told me the days and times the daughter and boyfriend worked, their address, and where to find the emergency key. On the surface, they didn't seem like lay about druggies to me, not with full-time jobs.

A small window of opportunity would be available with everyone at work or school, and I wanted to make sure that window was opened before going into the house.

"Hi. Would you tell Brenda . . . never mind. Could I just tell her something real quick? It'll only take a second."

Someone called for her, and she got on the line.

"Hello?"

"Hey, Brenda, can you tell . . . wait. This is Brenda, right? Brenda Stevens?"

"Yeah. Who's this?"

"Hey, can you tell Tommy I won't be able to . . ."

I hung up and dialed another number.

"Gary Smith Ford, how can we help you?"

"Can I speak with the service department, please?"

"Service."

"Hi. I need to bring my car in. Something's screwed up with the electrical, I think. My friend said you had a guy working for you, Tommy Buford? Said he was the best."

I heard a slight chuckle on the other end.

"I don't think it's Tommy your friend was talking about. He's not . . . well, I don't think it's him. Might be Dave, Dave Shepherd. He's pretty sharp."

"Well, is Tommy working today, in case I brought it in? My friend said he was good."

"Yeah. He'll be here till five."

I hung up the pay phone and drove to the CinemaPlex, left the van parked with the others, ran four miles to the house, positioned the cameras, did a quick search, and got out before the girl got home from school.

Whew . . .

They had some drugs - marihuana, cocaine, and what might be ecstasy – but nothing suggesting Tommy was a drug dealer, or they were anything but recreational users.

I moved to The Home Depot parking lot to hang around before leaving for the Hog's Breath Saloon to play my sets. The cameras were set up in the two bedrooms and the living room, and I watched in real time on the disposable phone.

The girl and boyfriend had been home for hours. There was little interaction between them but they appeared to get along. He watched television, and she listened to music through her headphones. I presumed it was music because her foot tapped like a metronome.

Other than a couple of times when the girl moved her arm after Tommy reached over and patted it, he hadn't tried to touch her. The girl's reaction could have been a typical *you're not my dad* gesture.

The mother wouldn't be home until nine-ish, so I tapped a button on the touchscreen and switched from *live feed* to *record* before heading to the Hog's Head.

During the break, I watched what I'd recorded.

Everything seemed fine.

Mom was home and all of them spent time together before the girl went to bed. The adults watched television. made some drinks, took some pills, lit up a doobie, and started to get frisky just as it came time to play my last set.

By the way, in case you were wondering, I was having a blast. The crowd was loud, and I was great. There was something about playing on the Hog's stage that brought out my best. I might have to move here.

With the show over and the van packed, I pulled up the live feed. It was very late or very early, depending on your perspective, and the house quiet and lit by nightlights.

The girl lay between the two of them in her mother's bed, a sweet picture of a sleeping family after a long day.

Except for everyone being naked.

I watched the video until I couldn't and then fast forwarded through the rest before switching back to real time. They hadn't moved an inch in two hours.

Probably because of the smoke and the drink, the pills and the cocaine they'd ingested – and I wanted to go over and put a bullet into both of their heads because they'd given that girl the same smoke, drink, pills, and coke, and used her repeatedly to satisfy themselves.

I was full of fury with murder in my heart as I pulled out of the parking lot and headed to their house. My natural inclination towards stillness in stressful situations was impaired, and I struggled to get a grip on my emotions.

The wickedness of that mother in the corruption of her daughter enraged me, and I couldn't find any calm until I thought of my own, sleeping safe and sound and needing me to help guide and protect her.

There was too much risk in killing them tonight, for me and the girl, and I needed to think before I acted.

Elisabeth knew I'd care about Naomi's fear and hoped I'd investigate her allegations because, if they were true, she knew I'd kill the boyfriend. That's why she'd called me.

But how would she feel if I killed her friend's daughter? Would she turn me in to the police? Would Naomi? I couldn't trust they'd let me do what needed doing - send Brenda to hell. I couldn't trust anyone with that.

Except Mary.

I'd pull the cameras from the house tomorrow and consider how best to give Elisabeth the information. Maybe I'd stop and see her before we left for St. Vincent. I turned the van around and headed back to my family, girl and dog.

~~

I tried to leave Mary at the hotel in the morning, willing to pay for another night to cover the time I'd be gone. But when she balked, there were only two choices available – not tell her and insist that she stayed, or . . .

"I want to invoke a *don't ask, don't tell.*"

She raised her brows, eyes filled with interest.

"I'd also like to attach a favor, if you'd consider it."

"Nothing to consider, Dax. If you need it, it's yours."

"You're a good kid, you know that?"

"Yup."

I did a quick but subtle look around and walked to the porch, used the hidden key, and opened the door with the sleeve of my sweatshirt. After gathering the cameras, I then went to the back door.

Yesterday, I'd seen a path through a lightly wooded area. It led to the next street where I'd asked Mary to meet me five minutes after dropping me a block away. She said it wasn't much of a favor but had a sparkle in her eyes, relishing the opportunity to drive illegally in broad daylight.

I slid the hoodie over my head, opened the door and left. Mary pulled up just as I cleared the trees. I asked if she wanted to drive home, and she asked if I'd really let her.

"Do you think you could? It's ninety-some miles."

"Sure, if I had to."

"Good to know. Now scooch over, sweetie."

I was proud of her for abiding by the spirit of the *don't ask, don't tell* precept. She didn't look at me about it or make a comment. I hoped she didn't invoke her own someday over a boy. Coincidentally, she looked over with a trace of what I thought might be a glimmer of glee in her eyes but that couldn't be right. She'd have to be reading my mind.

Are you reading my mind, little girl? I thought at her.

Her expression didn't change as she turned back to watch the scenery, but I saw a hint of a smile.

"Mare?"

"Yeah?"

"Are you?"

"Are I what, Dax?"

I didn't say another word and neither did she as she kept looking out her window. I smiled in fascination, but it was short-lived as I considered how to help that poor girl.

I'd decided not to talk to Elisabeth Dobson. The less she knew the better, and I couldn't let her interfere in what I had to do – save the girl by killing her mother. I thought about talking to Naomi but didn't know how she'd respond.

Would she go to the police and tell them what was going on, knowing what would happen to her daughter?

Would she save the life of her granddaughter if it meant her daughter's life would be forfeited?

Would she be strong enough to handle the emotional turmoil, take care of the girl and leave her daughter to her fate? If not, would the girl end up going from foster home to foster home, maybe being abused along the way?

And if I sent the video to the police?

Would some perversion of the justice system allow the boyfriend and mother to walk free?

Would they kill her if they had the chance, to keep her from testifying against them?

Would the girl have enough love and support to survive the madness of her mother's betrayal if the video got out?

A clear path to her salvation was difficult to see, and that might be from fatigue. I was bone-tired and already imagining my head hitting the pillow with fifty miles to go. I hated the idea of her spending another night with those people, but I needed to think. And to do that properly, I had to get some sleep.

"Want to take the helm, girl?"

The surprise in her eyes gave way to eagerness. She nodded, smiled, and nodded again.

"And to make it interesting, I'm going to take a nap. Still want it?" I could see her factoring this variable by the way she looked up and to her right.

"If I get us home without killing us, can I get my license? There's a class starting next week."

"Well, you'd get a learner's permit first, but, yes. *If* you don't kill us. Otherwise the deal is off," I said, pulling over and switching seats.

After checking her mirrors, she eased into traffic and drove down the road.

"Make sure to stay below the speed limit, hon, and watch your blind spots." I positioned myself in the seat and closed my eyes with sleep only minutes away.

"I can't wait to take Paul out for a ride," she said quietly.

See what I mean about that button?

"Eyes on the road, smartass."

Mary saw him grin and it made her smile. Truth was, Dax didn't have anything to worry about. Her feelings about sex hadn't changed, she wasn't having any for a long while. But he didn't know that, and she was having too much fun to ease his mind. Maybe someday.

She thought of one of the reasons for her abstinence, grateful that *sonofabitch* had used protection – though she knew his decision had nothing to do with her and everything to do with protecting himself. She'd never think of that man as a father again. He was a rapist, a molester of children, an evil abomination, and every day he spent underground was a *damned good one.*

Her thoughts turned to Dax's *don't ask, don't tell*, which wasn't a request but a notification. Neither had used one before, and she knew its invoking was caused by her wanting to leave the hotel rather than stay. He could have insisted but instead asked for her help.

The trust he showed by including her meant as much as the honesty they shared, and the river of her love and respect ran deep and true.

chapter twenty

We invited Tasha to join us for dinner at the Sunset Grill in town, and I smiled at how the little girl in Mary came out every now and then when they were together. I'd seen more of Tasha's too, and sometimes they acted like kids, laughing and playing without a care in the world.

I'd thought about the girl in Destin all day. A perfect solution didn't exist, or if it did, I couldn't see it. My options were limited because of Elisabeth, and the best I could do for that girl right now, was send the video of her abuse to the authorities in the morning.

The police would contact the grandmother who might be the girl's only hope of surviving her experience. I'd like to help Naomi with that, but I couldn't have any contact with her because someday, I was going to kill her daughter. Someday soon. And it wasn't going to be pretty or quick.

"I'm sorry, what?"

Mary looked at me and shook her head.

"I said, do you want to play for a while? We can all go back to the house, make some music, tell some jokes, and have a few drinks."

I raised my brow and looked over at Tasha.

"Drinks?"

"Why not? We're all adults here."

I smiled and so did Tasha.

"Adults, you say. We? We all are? Enlighten me."

Mary's eyes shimmered.

"Well, the definition of an adult is a fully grown human, and, as you can see, I have definitely grown fully," she said, sticking out her chest. "The definition also states you're an adult when you've reached the age of maturity, and Dax, you're always telling me I'm very mature. How I'm the most mature young lady you've ever known."

She looked from Dax to Tasha.

"Now, Mare . . ."

"She's right, Dax. I've heard you say it many times. And you always seem so proud of her when you do."

"Tasha, I . . ."

"Wait. Didn't you mean it? Dax? Were you just saying that?" Mary asked with hitch in her eyes and breath.

"Mare, don't . . ."

"Did you . . ."

"Mary, I . . ."

"Dax? Did you lie to me?"

A tug pulled on my heart strings when I saw the misting in her eyes that would coalesce into tears.

"Oh, that's a nice touch. You're wide-eye is getting better and better."

She let one drop before bursting into laughter, causing the other dinner guests to look over. Tasha and I shared the moment with them and some returned a smile.

"I thought you might crack for a second," Mary said.

"No way. But, please don't do that again, okay? Even for fun. It just . . . It breaks my heart to think of your being disappointed in me, Mare. It . . . I can't . . ." My voice broke, and I looked away before lowering my head.

"Oh, Dax. I'm sorry. Please, I . . ."

I looked up with a grin and collected my prize.

"You, big shit," she said.

Tasha cracked up and looked them over. "You two just kill me. Don't ever stop."

We reveled in the relationship we'd created.

"Mare, didn't you forget something in the recitation of your definition? It says, 'When a human has reached the *legal* age of maturity.'"

"I didn't forget. I omitted," she said. "And I was just kidding about drinking. Although, I used to make a pretty good mojito." Her smile weakened as she remembered why.

"So what about it, guys? Want to do the music *thang*," she asked again, giving the last word a country twang.

I cocked my head and Tasha nodded.

"I'll have to go home, first. Be at your place in an hour?"

~~

James smiled at the ease with which he'd bypassed the security measures by simply walking around them. He tripped the *red-eye* alarm and waited for them to respond, but they didn't.

Or wouldn't.

Stepping by the last warning device, he stopped inside the tree line some thirty yards away from the house and threw a stick towards it. The bright light failed to shine. He waited thirty seconds and threw another toward the side which also remained dark after the branch landed.

The motion detectors were either off or defective, and it worked to his advantage. However, there didn't seem to be any indication anyone was home – no shadows of movement, no sound from a television, no barking dog, not even an occasional light turning on or off.

He knew in his gut they were gone, and it pissed him off. He'd driven too far and wanted her too much, so he put on the buff to cover his face and proceeded to the secondary plan - get inside and surprise them when they came home.

As he stepped out into the clearing, he heard the pump-action of a shotgun and fell to his chest just before the buckshot struck the trees over his head. He lay still as another shell was loaded.

"I won't miss next time. Better get up and skedaddle."

After a minute, he rolled on his back to check his front. He wasn't hit, as far as he knew, and blew a sigh of relief as he looked at the night sky.

He noticed some paper flapping in the breeze on the backside of a tree and saw more paper on other trees with barely noticeable wiring rising from the ground.

"Son of a bitch. Palmer is using squibs," he said, not laughing, not smiling, not appreciating the simple elegance of this 'get off my property' solution. James didn't find any humor in falling for this silly bit of subterfuge. Instead, he thought of killing Palmer in a gruesome manner and forcing Mary to watch before killing her dog as well.

Won't be so fucking funny then, will it?

He cursed Kevin for failing to include this information in his surveillance report and moved toward the house, ready to draw his gun and shoot anything that moved. The sprinkler shot him first. He was covered in paint and gas in seconds making it almost impossible to see. Not knowing what other booby-traps were in place, he turned and went back to the car. His eyes stung, and his clothes stank and stuck to his skin as anger rose with the bile.

James spat whispered invectives about what he'd do to Kevin, to Palmer – and to Mary.

~~

Eric Clapton's, *I Shot the Sheriff,* started playing as soon as I cranked up the truck. My phone informed me that the *black-eye* alarm had been triggered. I tapped the screen but didn't see anyone on the live feed, so I pulled up the video. A man walked into the open before dropping quickly to the ground to avoid the 'buckshot.'

I never tired of seeing that.

Since Mary's whereabouts became known, there'd been seventeen incidents of trespassing that triggered the simulated shotgun and nine that triggered the sprinklers.

They split almost evenly between people working for news organizations, people trying to get a picture to sell, and others who were curious and wanted a glimpse of Mary. Three of the curious were former classmates of hers from high school. All but one of all of them had done their trespassing during the daytime. Well, two now. I watched him get up, get sprayed, and then leave.

I didn't see a camera, but the guy was probably going to use his phone to take any pictures he hoped to sell. He wore a fishing buff, covering all but his eyes. The buff was a new twist but the reason for it wasn't. Other's also hid their faces to remain unidentifiable.

It had been a couple of weeks since anyone received a 'black eye,' and I showed the video to Mary who shook her head. We both got a kick out of seeing the paint find its mark and leave the person a total mess.

I'd had to modify the amount streaming through the sprinklers, thinning it so less was left on the driveway to find its way into the garage. Washing off the truck and shoveling gravel over the gas-paint mess was the price I paid for having my security fun. I'd have to put out more squibs tomorrow. Usually, four rounds were set, but the buff man had used up the last of them.

I shut off the alarms and turned down the driveway to the house with the window down, gun by my side, and Mary behind me. It was just a precaution because of the darkness. She didn't even roll her eyes when I asked her to lay on the cargo seat in the back.

She gets it. You live your life, do what you want, but stay alert and be prepared for the evil that people can do. Because it only takes one moment of complacency to change your life. Or kill you.

I didn't really think that man would still be around, but caution was a commodity I had plenty of. The smell of gas permeated the air as I drove into the clearing and onto the ramp I'd built for spraying the tires and undercarriage. I picked up the gun and punched the remote to open the garage door. After a quick look around, I got out of the truck.

"We're good. Let's go in and clear the house."

I handed Mary the smaller gun, watched her flip the safety off and take point. She continued to impress me with her calmness, and I was as proud as any parent ever was.

When we reached the garage and the door inside, I held back and observed. She approached confidently but carefully and listened through the door before knocking – one, one-two, one, one-two, two. Watson gave the same bark he always did when he heard it.

Mary opened the door, and I held the gun up and ready as she scratched Watson and asked if everything was okay. He nodded, and we went room by room looking for an intruder until all was clear. I didn't expect to find anyone, but this was a cautionary exercise Mary always enjoyed. She flipped the safety on and handed over the gun.

"Hang on to it. I have to go outside and throw some gravel first, but would you like to practice the '*home alone*' scenario before Tasha gets here?"

Mary grinned and glistened. She loved this kind of role playing. It was fun and instructive.

"I'll start after I shovel. Sound good?"

She nodded, and I turned toward the door.

"Oh, because we're pressed for time, would you mind asking Watson to wait in the bedroom? I'd like to run through it without your having to factor in another's safety. Just you and your opponent."

Watson looked at me like I took food from his bowl.

"I know, boy. I'll make it up to you," I said and left.

The mound of gravel sat by the driveway and I dug in. About five scoops from calling it done, something that felt like a truck hit me in the back, knocking me down and out.

~~

Tasha took the shower she'd needed to take earlier before meeting Dax and Mary at the Sunset Grill after a long, sweaty day out and about with people, perps, and painters.

One of the more interesting incidents occurred when she responded to a call from the small airport at the end of Jones Homestead road. Squeezed between two large men sat one petite woman, a college student taking classes at Gulf Coast Community College a few miles away.

She was four-foot seven and barely a hundred pounds, and Tasha extended her hand.

"Chica Sanguine, I presume. It is a pleasure to meet you," she said and thanked the men who'd detained her.

Tasha asked her to step outside, and they sat and watched the paint dry on the hangar exhibiting her mural.

"Miss Sanguine, I'm a big fan of your work. You're very good, and not just what you draw and your use of color. I especially like what you're saying about law enforcement."

"Rivera. My name is Maria Rivera. Chica is my tag name. What is it you think I'm trying to say?" she asked, looking boldly at Tasha, who was taking the measure of Maria. She was tough and feisty with the energy and righteousness of youth.

180

"You're reminding us that we are here to protect and serve the public, not to serve and protect ourselves. You'd like us to get our priorities in order."

Maria considered Tasha. Some of the edge was gone from her voice when she said, "Anything else?"

"Yeah. That guy in front of the Trading Post makes a helluva good doughnut, but everybody loves them. Not just the cops," she said, bringing a smile to Maria's face.

"So, Miss Rivera. Do you need to be arrested to make your point, or can we find another way to express yourself?"

Maria agreed to stop spraying commercial property and Tasha agreed to help find more suitable canvases for her art, wondering how her captain would react to a request to paint a mural on the police station walls.

Tasha stepped out of the shower and got ready to go have fun with her friends.

~~

Mary waited in the dark for Dax to begin the exercise, which was, an intruder comes into your house in the middle of the night after cutting the electricity. What do you do?

She had the gun, but knew he'd probably disarm her. Dax was quiet and quick, and she hadn't kept hold of it in the three times they'd run this simulation, requiring her to use other offensive solutions during the confrontation.

She'd stuck a pencil into his shoulder once when he pinned her on the floor with an arm across her throat. It was early in her training, and she hadn't yet learned to control her feelings, to think before you act. That pencil had been planted out of pure instinct.

Dax had praised her initiative, using it as a lesson in control, and she'd become more adept at quieting the fear and thinking her way through a conflict.

Mary checked her watch and wondered if this was a new tactic of his – uneasy anticipation. Knowing something was coming but not knowing when. She could appreciate how it might be unnerving and started to feel antsy herself. She went to the window and looked through the drapes. Dax was lying on the ground by the gravel pile.

Well, that's different.

Mary opened the door ready to call out, but the words caught in her throat. A man wearing a buff that covered his face stepped out from behind a tree, pointed a gun at Dax, and waved her over. She tried to calm the fear but couldn't, until she brought the gun up and pointed it at the man.

He knelt down and put the barrel of the suppressor to Dax's head. "Drop the gun, Mary, and come here."

She walked over with the gun still aimed at the man and stopped ten feet away. His eyes were familiar, but she didn't know why. Dax was still alive, but the wound in his back was weeping.

"Drop the gun, Mary."

"No."

James smiled at how strong she tried to be and was thrilled by the prospect of breaking her newfound spirit.

"Drop the gun, or I'll kill him."

"If you do, I'll blow your head off."

The smile on James' face disappeared, and his eyes reflected his surprise.

"I mean it, Mary. I'll kill him. Believe it."

A panic touched her heart, and he saw it in her eyes. Then he saw something else.

"I believe you. And the moment you move your finger, your gun, or any part of yourself I perceive as threatening, I'll empty the clip into you. Do you believe *me*?" she said and looked him stone-cold in the eyes, ready to shoot.

Holy shit, he thought.

He'd expected to find a broken little girl but instead found himself looking at a tiger looking at him. It was inconceivable that he could die at the hands of the girl he'd come to kidnap. He looked at the gun and saw the safety off, her finger on the trigger, her hand steady as a rock.

"Here are your options as I see them," Mary said. "Take the gun off Dax, point it at me, and stand up. Otherwise, I'm just going to shoot you and be done with it."

"You'll be killing him. Can you live with that? I thought you cared about him."

"I do, but *I* won't be killing him. You will. Then I'll kill *you*. I can live with that. Can you?"

Mary recognized she'd had another break from herself, another dissociative state where the person speaking and pointing the gun had stepped in to help the girl who was too afraid for Dax, who would have done whatever the man wanted, hoping against reason and logic he wouldn't kill him if she complied. That girl knew she was a liability so she'd moved aside and let Mary do what had to be done.

James was sweating under the buff, realizing his choices were indeed limited and the rest of his life could be counted in seconds. There wasn't a doubt in his mind this little bitch was going to shoot him dead.

"I'm moving my gun to you," he said and considered shooting her in the leg as he swung his arm.

"Sure you want to do that?

James was thrown by her rock-solid intuition and stood up less sure of himself than he'd been two seconds ago.

"What do you want? Why are you here?"

"I'm here for you, Mary. I want you to come with me."

"Why?"

He didn't answer.

Mary did the calculations. While feasible, there was too much risk he might kill Dax before she could kill him, regardless of who shot first. As long as he wanted her, for whatever reason, she could use that to draw him away. If she went with him, Dax would have a chance.

"Now what?" he asked, astounded he was under the gun and negotiating with a kid.

"We could shoot each other now and get it over with, or I could leave with you," she said and stepped toward the driveway with the gun pointed steadily on his face.

James moved with her, gun held in place trying to convince her he'd shoot but knowing he wouldn't by choice. He wanted her in his trunk.

Half-way down the driveway, Mary stopped and looked at eyes she knew but didn't.

"Why do you want me?" she asked, committed to killing and being killed in order to save Dax.

He took off the buff and smiled.

"I know you, Mary. I know what you want. I've seen you with your father and . . ."

In a flash, she saw a way. Her gun lowered slightly.

"My father? Where is he? Is he alright? Are you here to take me to him?" she asked in wide-eyed desperation to find him, to be with him.

James was utterly confused. In an instant, the tiger became a cub, wanting to be with her father, needing to be.

He shook his head, and she looked distraught.

"Who are you? Your eyes . . ."

"I'm his brother. Your uncle."

He watched her lower the gun to her side, wary about the change in her demeanor.

"I didn't know he had a brother," she said, telling the truth. Her eyes filled with hope and her voice cracked when she asked. "Do you know where he is? I . . . I miss him."

James saw her blush as she looked straight at him and shook his head again, pondering the strange turn of events. "Why are you here? Why didn't you go with your father?"

"I ran away. I got mad and told him I'd tell. Dax found me and took me in."

"What would you tell?" he asked, trying to gauge her sincerity. Mary looked confused.

"You said you saw us. Me and my father."

"Only a picture he sent," James said, lying to expose the truth. "Tell me what happened."

"He, uh . . . he did things. And I . . . I, uh . . ." Mary looked away, embarrassed.

James was now more curious than cautious, wanting her to say it and believing she wanted to.

"He touched you?"

She nodded, still looking away.

"And did you like it? Did you like to be touched?"

James was drawn to her and became aroused, almost forgetting she had a gun in his need to hear it from her.

"He . . . forced himself. I didn't want it. It was wrong. But then, I . . ." she said quietly.

James saw the exquisite humiliation of her surrender.

"Did you want him to touch you, Mary? To take you?" he asked, his voice almost a whisper.

Mary looked deep inside of him, eyes full of disgrace but tinged with want.

"Yes. I . . . yes."

Her face burned with shame, and James brushed his cool fingers against the heat of it before tracing them down her arm in a slow caress. When he reached her hand, she let him take the gun and throw it into the woods. He moved behind her and spoke softly as the barrel of his own rested against her cheek.

"Would you like that, Mary? To be taken? To give in to your desire?" He grabbed a handful of her hair, and she leaned back willingly, pressing against him.

Here we go, Mary thought, coming to the epicenter of her escape after arranging the advantage she would exploit. She was optimally positioned with the added bonus of not having to look at him as he touched her.

Mary pressed again and was rewarded with a groan. He fondled her breast, and she let loose an expulsion of breath, prompting him to put his hand under her shirt. He took the gun from her face when he put his arm across her chest and pushed himself against her.

"Yessss," she whispered convincingly. His hand moved downward, and Mary helped give him access by widening her stance, causing him to widen his own. When he reached his destination, she moaned as deeply as she ever had..

He groaned in pleasure and then groaned in pain after Mary quickly brought the heel of her foot up between his legs and found her target. The back of her head cracked his nose and his hand pulled free.

She took hold of the arm across her chest and bit down hard, spinning out and away from his grasp. Wiping the blood from her mouth, she looked around for something to strike him with.

When he swung the gun around, she ducked inside and caught him by surprise, hitting him with her shoulder and knocking him to the ground. He dropped the gun but grabbed her arms and twisted his body when she brought a knee to his crotch. She immediately tried to smash his nose again, but he moved his head just in time and rolled her over and sat on top, stretching her arms high above her head.

"You little bitch. I can't wait to get you to the cabin. I'll do things to you my brother never dreamed of. And when I'm done, I'll give you to a hundred men and . . ."

She watched the fire in his eyes burn with anger, lust, power, depravity, and saw what Dax must see – the endless evil and the need to eradicate it.

He was just out of reach, so she turned away in disgust and opened a dialog.

"I hope you'll at least brush your teeth or use a breath mint before you do me, asshole. You stink."

James was incensed and shoved his face at hers.

"You think you're a tough little shit, but you're just . . ."

Mary lifted her head and clamped down. He tried to pull away, and then let go of a wrist and hit her repeatedly. She held on tight, closed her eyes when the blood fell, felt it give when he jerked back, and spit the nose on the ground. James screamed in pain and hatred and began to choke her, putting his full weight into it.

"You, cunt! You want to die? Shit, no problem," he said, pressing harder and harder and watching her eyes bulge. He barely saw Mary's hand moving but quickly understood the reason for it when something plunged into his eye.

She coughed and struggled for breath when he let her go and pushed him off when she could. He thrashed about on the ground trying, with bloody fingers, to dislodge the ink pen she'd buried deep, the pen she put in her pocket when she'd thought about that pencil. A yellow pen with green writing from Scallop Cove Bait and Tackle.

Mary stood over him, assessing the situation, looking for weakness in her opponent, an advantage to exploit. She lifted her foot and drove the pen into his brain with the heel of her shoe, driving it over and over until long after her father had stopped moving.

She picked up his gun and raised a hand to shield her eyes from the light coming down the driveway.

"Mary! What . . ." Tasha jumped out of the truck.

"Hang on," she said, and put three quiet bullets into his head. Tasha was stunned and unable to speak until Mary rolled the man off the driveway into the brush.

"Mary, please. What's going on?"

She looked at Tasha.

"Dax has been shot."

After they checked on him and called for an EMS bus, Mary went into the house and came out with the gun, a flashlight, and a dog. When Tasha asked where she was headed, she said she'd be right back.

"Mary, please. Stay here, I'll go. What do you need? Where are you going?"

"I need to find something first, then I'll tell you. Please stay with Dax. Don't let him die," she said, and walked up the driveway with Watson beside her.

She later returned with a phone in her back pocket, and a laptop tucked under her arm, telling Tasha she intended to look for videos before giving them to the authorities.

Mary said she'd found his vehicle but didn't have to break the window because the *asshole* left it unlocked. She'd also found a plastic crypt meant for her after she popped the trunk to look inside.

When Tasha asked about the extra gun stuck into the waist of her pants, Mary told her everything, leaving no detail unsaid.

After commending her bravery, Tasha asked if she'd be comfortable with altering the facts. Not because she'd done anything wrong, on the contrary, she'd done everything right. But Tasha thought if she left out the gun Dax had given her and the sexual element of her attack when talking to investigators, it might take the focus off of her sooner, rather than later.

Especially when the story broke in the news.

Mary had already made that decision. That's why she'd gone to find her gun – so she wouldn't have to answer, 'why didn't you shoot him with the gun in your hand' questions. And she most certainly wasn't going to tell anyone about what she'd done and why.

What bothered her most was how Dax would respond to her solution.

"He'll be proud of the way you handled yourself and the quick thinking you displayed under extreme duress," Tasha told her.

"Maybe, but he's not going to be happy I put myself in danger. He'll say I should have shot that man dead when he had the gun against his head."

Mary teared up, finding it difficult to continue.

"But how could I have done that? I couldn't let Dax die. I... I can't lose him," she said, falling into Tasha's arms. She held on until the ambulance pulled up beside them, bathing them in red and yellow light.

chapter twenty-one

He was later identified as Robert James Thompson, stepbrother of John Stewart and current Assistant Deputy-Director of the Sex Trafficking division in the Atlanta field office of the FBI. He'd been a participant in the sex trade he was tasked to uncover and eliminate, using his position to protect those involved and helping facilitate their activities.

"He was literally the fox in the henhouse," Jeri said

~

Tasha had helped Mary while Dax recuperated in the hospital, acting as a buffer between law enforcement's need for information and Mary's need for protection and privacy.

Mary told investigators the man said he would kill Dax, whom he'd already shot in the back, if she didn't come with him. When they were walking up the driveway, he told her who he was and why he was taking her. When she stopped, he grabbed her by the hair from behind. That's when she fought back, eventually shooting him in the head with his gun, making sure he was dead.

Tasha sat through the interviews with Mary, marveling at her composure, and her ability to tell such a believable lie with such a straight and believable face.

~

The girl in Destin was dead.

She'd cut her wrists, two hours after I'd collected the hidden cameras. She hadn't left a note.

My face was wet when Mary returned from the hospital cafeteria, but I didn't say why or what was wrong. I just held her hand, patting and rubbing and thinking.

~

Watson stuck close to Mary. Maybe a little too close because she'd tripped over him twice already.

'That's gonna happen when you lock me in a room and almost get yourself killed,' he'd told her.

She explained how it happened, and how she wouldn't have had time to let him out even if she'd thought about him.

His feelings were hurt until she said it actually worked out for the best, because that man would have killed him if he'd tried to save her. When he said it was his job to protect her, she said it was also hers to protect him.

"Well, at least think about me the next time."

"You mean the next time someone shoots Dax in the back and tries to kidnap me?" she said with a grin.

He smiled back and asked for a scratch.

"Oh yeah, right there."

~~

"Dr. Pepper alright?"

"Yeah, thanks," I said, sitting in the big chair a few days after leaving the hospital. The bullet hadn't caused as much damage as it could have, but I might not have been shot in the first place if I'd paid more attention.

I tried to be fair in my assessment but couldn't shake the feeling I'd screwed up and put her in danger. It kept coming back to my inability to consider he might return after being sprinkled. But how could I have known he was coming for her, specifically and purposefully?

"Exactly," Mary said as she put the Pepper on a coaster in front of me and sat on the couch.

"What?"

"What?" she asked.

"Why are you what-ing me? You said something."

"Did I?"

I watched her sip sweet tea and again contemplated her potential mind reading capabilities. She looked at me as innocently as anyone who had nothing to hide. I winced when my arm bumped against the armrest. I hadn't wanted to take the prescribed pain pills, but I'd need them tonight.

"I'm sorry, Mare."

"For?"

When I told her, she said, "If he was coming for me, it could have been at any time, on any day or night, right?

Can't blame yourself for something you couldn't foresee. You see?"

I liked the succinct way she'd gotten to the truth of it.

"Unless, of course, you knew he was coming to get me. Then yeah, you screwed up. Did you know, Dax?" she asked, a little wide-eye up and working.

"Ha-ha," I said, finally ready to ask her.

"Was it hard to let him touch you? To pretend you wanted him to?" I'd been worried about old feelings being stirred up and relived.

"It was harder to pretend than to be touched. Acting that way and saying those things was perverse. But thanks to good-old-dead dad, I knew what that man wanted to hear and how he wanted me to be. It was the only way I could think of to give me a chance to get through it alive," she said, and then looked at me for real.

"Because I was going to kill him, Dax, regardless of what happened to me."

I saw the depth of her sincerity and nodded.

"Yeah, about that. Instead of shooting him when his gun was pointed at me, you put your life at risk, and it's been bothering me. I've been thinking a lot about it, trying to find a way to . . . I don't know, chastise you?" I said, holding up my hand when she started to speak.

"But Mare, you did everything I would have if the roles were reversed, except I wouldn't have been as quick in finding a solution as effective as you did. I would have tried, and I would have killed him for sure, but . . ."

I didn't need to tell her what she already knew; I could have been killed in the trying. Just like she could have.

"I forget, sometimes, that you're as protective of me as I am of you, and I can't fault your decision to risk your life for mine. You did great, sweetie, and I'm very proud of you."

Mary's eyes misted, and she nodded when I thanked her for saving my life.

"Thanks for saving mine, too," she said.

I returned her nod, and we shared the moment before I changed the topic to keep from tearing up.

"There is a question I have, though. Why didn't you put a couple between his legs? You know, for the hell of it?"

She smiled and shook her head.

"That's on you. Next time, stop lazing around on the ground and bleeding out. Give a girl a chance to finish what she started."

Knockin' on Heaven's Door played through the speakers when the gate opened. Tasha tripped the other electronic eyes - *Green Onion, Yellow Submarine,* and *Red House,* as she drove up the driveway.

She was coming to take Mary and Watson out on the boat and later to her house for a sleep-over, giving me an opportunity to relax and rest from gunshot and surgery.

"Sure you'll be okay by yourself? I can stay."

"Thanks, but I'll be fine. If I get restless, I might go for a drive down the coast, feel the breeze. Maybe get out and wade in the water."

She looked at me like she knew damned well what I was going to do and cocked her head the way Watson did when he asked if I was crazy.

"Dax?"

"Yeah?"

"Be careful when you wade out in the water. Okay?"

"I will, hon."

~~

They both caught a 'slam' – trout, redfish, and flounder. Mary caught the biggest fish, but Tasha caught the most. They kept two flounder for dinner and released the rest.

Watson jumped into the water and caught a turtle, but Tasha told him he couldn't keep it. He played with it for a few minutes before Mary said a shark might come by and play with him, too. He smiled, said *Funny*, and then casually swam to the boat and waited to be hauled aboard.

They left for her house and dinner before sunset. When Tasha put some wine into a glass, Mary looked at her, then to an empty glass, then back to Tasha with a smile on her face and a sparkle in her eyes.

"Don't even try that with me, girl. I am immune to your sweet and innocent charms. I would, however, give you a little Chardonnay with your dinner if you don't think Dax would mind. Or, you don't tell on me if he would," Tasha said with a grin and a wink.

They spent the night talking and laughing - about Dax, about each other, even about Watson who'd found a place on a living room rug to lay down. He fell asleep before the conversation turned serious.

The two of them drew closer to each other and shared their thoughts and lives. Tasha told Mary about her father, what he'd done, what she'd done, and the nightmares that had tormented her for years. They cried and hugged and bonded over shared experiences, feeling like sisters.

"I want you to know how important you've become to me, Mary. You and Dax," Tasha said, pouring more wine into their glasses. "And how special I think the two of you are. I'm so grateful for your friendship."

Tasha was amazed at how close she felt to Mary, given her age, but she was mature beyond her years, an adult living in a teenager's body.

I probably shouldn't be giving her wine, though.

"Why not?"

"What? Did I say that out loud?"

Mary nodded. Tasha grinned and swirled the yellow liquid in her glass before taking a sip.

"I was thinking about how mature you are, not like a teenager at all, but like an adult, and I've been talking to you most of the night as if you were one. And filling your glass as if you were as well. Dax is going to be upset with me."

Mary gave Tasha a grin and a twinkle.

"Well, I like how you treat me as an adult. I also like how, sometimes, you act like a teenager. And I've only had two and a half glasses over a four-hour period, so you're not exactly contributing to the delinquency."

Tasha grimaced but Mary's grin made her laugh, and she let it go.

"And unless Dax asks me specifically if you gave me wine with my fish dinner, I won't have to tell him you did."

"What do you mean?"

Mary told her about the honesty between them, how it worked, and how much it meant to them. Tasha smiled when she mentioned *respectful declinations*.

"Isn't it just the same as saying yes or no?"

"Sometimes, but it's excepted as a legitimate response without reproach. We don't ask questions unless we're prepared to hear the truth, and we always have the right not to answer. But if we do, we never lie."

Tasha was intrigued.

"Huh. So, if Dax started to wear a comb-over and asked if he looked silly, you wouldn't just say, 'No, you look fine?" Tasha asked. "To spare his feelings?"

"Well, if he didn't look silly, I'd luck out, wouldn't I? Then I could say no." Mary raised an eyebrow and grinned.

"And if he did?"

"I might try to use humor to avoid having to hurt his feelings, see if that might curtail his need to know. But if he insisted, I'd give it to him straight rather than respectfully decline to answer. He'd respect that."

Tasha nodded and said, "So, if he didn't want his feelings hurt, he probably wouldn't ask if he looked silly."

"Well, he wouldn't ask *me*."

Tasha chuckled.

"I like you, Mary. You're interesting and funny."

"I like you, too, Tasha. I think you're interesting, too."

"What? You don't think I'm funny?"

Mary's eyes filled with merriment.

~~

I gazed at the magnificence of the milky way - the galaxy, not the candy bar - and considered my place in the universe and my small contribution to its glory.

Which was really non-existent in the context of celestial bodies moving about in the vacuum of space. Those stars were going to turn and burn, unknowing and uncaring about our small blue ball and the good people who lived and died upon it striving to make a better world.

Maybe I didn't contribute at all? I didn't plant trees or flowers, nor did I seed or maintain the lush grass that felt so good between the toes. I didn't nourish the landscape or sculpt it to be both functional and pleasing to the eye.

I just killed the weeds.

As I waded in the water, I grinned thinking I wasn't only killing weeds. I was helping a young tree grow strong and tall. Maybe I should stop pulling weeds and just nurture that tree?

But what about the others? Those who were alive and needed help, and those who were dead and needed justice?

I loved Mary, and if the choice was between her well-being and the well-being of strangers, I'd choose her, always. But the suffering of people I could have helped and didn't would weigh heavily on me, as would knowing their suffering would continue and go unpunished.

It was a conundrum I didn't have an answer for at the moment, but I knew one thing for certain – that mother and her boyfriend had not gone unpunished. And the reason that girl killed herself would be known to everyone when their bodies were discovered, and the DVD was found.

I could have let them be, hoped a friend or classmate of hers came forward with some information or the police stumbled onto the truth. I could have sent the video and hoped the system did right by that dead and abused girl.

Yeah . . . no.

Those two had to go, and I'd found a way to get it done with little fuss and no muss.

The easiest way would have been to use the key. Wait for them to come home from work, shoot each in the head as they walked through the door, and then leave the video of what they'd done to that child in her hand.

Here's what they did, and here's why they're dead. Simple and direct.

But it wasn't that simple, because I didn't know what Elisabeth might have said to her friend. And either one of them could point the police at me, leapfrogging over suspicion and observation and landing directly on scrutiny and complication.

You know how I feel about that.

Except for killing Jefferson Dobson in a hurry and on the fly, the others were eliminated only after careful consideration and planning. I'd find something in their lives or routines that lent itself to their demise.

The same was true with Tommy and Brenda. They were sexual predators who used drugs and alcohol, with a drawer full of toys and sexually explicit videos on the entertainment center in their bedroom, most of them rape and bondage, dominance and submission.

I *did* end up using the key but, instead of putting a bullet in their heads, I compelled them to indulge themselves.

One died violently and the other from natural cause – cause of the something I made them take with their pills. A time-released something that didn't go well with the scotch, the meth-amphetamine laced cocaine, the ecstasy, and the strenuous sexual activity they'd been engaged in.

One was restrained and the other wasn't, but both derived pleasure from their respective roles and positions.

Toward the end, while they were so engaged, I played the DVD for them, the one the police would find showing what they'd done to their girl. Seeing and hearing her on the big screen television didn't slow them down at all, in fact their passion seemed to intensify.

They were depraved and indifferent, and I almost shot em' dead. But, I let them finish. And then I finished *them*.

I left the chair and placed the remote and the butcher knife on the bed. He was glassy eyed and slow, looking at me in a haze of thought, unclear and unfocused.

"Tommy, Brenda told me it was you that wanted Lisa, that you threatened to kill her if she didn't give her to you. Said you'd kill them both if they didn't do what you wanted."

Brenda said something, but her words were muffled by the duct tape, her head ensconced in a latex hood. She tried to move underneath Tommy, but he was heavy, and her hands were cuffed to a railing at the foot of the bed.

Tommy shook his head but only mumbled, not fully aware of what was happening or what he'd heard. When Brenda writhed, he groaned and started to move in and out of her in a state of perpetual arousal and erection caused by the drink, the drugs, and the Viagra I'd given him.

"Tommy, she said she was going to the police. That she was going to blame you, gonna tell them to lock you up."

"Fuuuckk, that. Shees the one want me to. Bitch, better shut fuck up. Kill her. I'll keeell her."

Brenda struggled and tried to talk, but it sounded like moaning and groaning. Tommy was pissed and excited. Still inside of her, he got on his knees, held her neck in one hand, and picked up the knife with the other. He winced in pain, the time-released something beginning to take effect.

In a few minutes, he'd be dead, they both would, but I wanted that mother to suffer.

"Tommy, she's going to tell everybody it was you and only you, and she's going to laugh when they take you away. Do you want that?"

Brenda was really bucking now, and Tommy pounded her harder and harder.

I reached down and pulled the hood from Brenda's head, seeing the fear in her eyes. Keeping the gun and an eye on Tommy,, I squatted and whispered in her ear. She became frantic, and I stood up and stepped back.

"Use the knife, Tommy. That'll shut her up. She won't be telling anybody anything if you use the knife. Will you, Brenda?"

She looked at me and then at Tommy as the knife plunged into her over and over, her muffled screams fueling his excitement, creating a vicious cycle until he was spent, and she was dead.

I tried to talk Tommy into opening the jugular vein on the side of his neck, but he didn't respond. Instead he moved in and out of his dead girlfriend until he cried out in pain, clutched his stomach, and fell to the floor.

In a couple minutes, he stopped breathing and I left.

The milky way shimmered and beckoned me to stay in the water and admire its beauty, but I needed to get home.

"Yes, you're beautiful," I said, stepping out of the Gulf and slipping into my sandals, pausing afterward to look at the night sky once more before I left

Was there a supreme being watching and waiting to judge and condemn me for my actions? If so, why didn't He step in and do something to help the people who needed it? Why didn't God protect and save that little girl?

If I was going to be judged, so was He.

Or She.

chapter twenty-two

We sat around the living room coffee table after dinner, coasters holding glasses filled with rootbeer and chardonnay. Tasha had been coming over quite a bit, so I always had wine chilling in the fridge. Kendall-Jackson was her favorite, but she drank wine from a box most of the time. She was a no-frills kind of girl.

I liked that.

Mary asked if she could have some wine, "just a taste, really," and I poured her a little. We all clinked our glasses together and smiled, feeling sophisticated. I even held my pinky finger up and out as I took a swig of my 'beer.'

A conversation that began about fishing meandered through a wide range of topics leading inexplicably to a discussion about vigilantism.

I listened to Tasha and Mary go over the pros and cons from different perspectives but with similar thoughts and beliefs. They agreed most people weren't capable of making decisions about fair and appropriate justice without their emotionalism interfering with their judgement. *Except for me*, they said at the same time and started laughing.

I laughed with them but spoke up when Tasha began to disparage revenge.

"Hang on. I think revenge has gotten a bad rap over the years. There's nothing wrong with it as long as it's just."

Tasha raised an eyebrow with surprise in her eyes. "You're not saying people should go out and kill each other, are you? Just take the law in their own hands and dispense a little frontier justice?"

"Well, no. And, yes. You both correctly identified one of the significant problems with street justice – the ease with which an individual allows their emotions to override the correctness of their certitude. It is imperative that all decisions are based on fact and fairness and not feelings, otherwise it's wrong and a mistake."

I saw a glint of agreement in Tasha's eyes and knew she was waiting for a *but*...

"However, if it's justified, there's nothing wrong with meting out punishment with a little righteous indignation, is there?" I smiled to give my words traction,.

"But Dax, we can't just let people make up their own minds about who lives and dies. It would be chaos and the innocent could be killed with the guilty."

Tasha hit the nail on the head.

"Exactly. It's not just that people can't keep their emotions in check, they also have differences determining what is fair and right. Killing your neighbor because their dog peed in your yard and killing them for murdering your child are at opposite ends of the spectrum, yet people constantly run the gamut between the two because what is or isn't appropriate, as it relates to punishment, depends on the individual. And therein lies the rub."

"They need to let the law handle it, Dax. Yes, there is deficiency and abuse in the justice system, and I know things can fall through the cracks and sometimes the guilty go free and unpunished. But it would be anarchy to let people make decisions for themselves. Don't you see that?"

Mary watched the exchange, curious and concerned that Tasha was getting worked up. I sensed the same thing, not even questioning how I knew what Mary was feeling.

"I agree, Tash. Wholeheartedly. People as a rule cannot be trusted to act responsibly. Vigilantism isn't for everyone. Most wouldn't do right by it."

"But you think some could?" Tasha asked.

The tone of the discussion had changed and lurking behind her hazel-green eyes was a question I probably didn't want to hear or answer. So I tried to keep it light.

"Well, you and Mary think you both could, yes?" I grinned, tipped my A&W and started to rock in the big chair.

Tasha recognized it for what it was, an opportunity to leave the conversation and move on to other things. She took a swallow from her glass, glanced at Mary and then back to Dax.

"Do you recall a news story about a man getting killed in Destin a while back? I think you were playing there that night," Tasha asked.

Well, well, well.

"Hmm. Should I remember?"

"He was stabbed with an icepick and shot in the head."

"Oh, yeah. That guy. He was sitting in a car, I think. In front of, what, an old girlfriend's place?"

She looked at me with interest and curiosity and I gave her the beginnings of a wide-eye, conveying some curiosity of my own.

Tasha's reaction to seeing Dax raise his eyebrows was to grin. She'd seen similar expressions on Mary's face and it made her think, *like father, like daughter*. It also made her just a smidgeon suspicious, although she didn't know why. Maybe the detective in her thought that expression could be hiding something.

"The Destin police speculate he might have been killed because he'd been beating his ex-wife for years. They suspected him of putting her in the hospital just a few days earlier. What do you think of that?"

Mary asked if we wanted our glasses refilled and left for the kitchen when we said *yes*.

"Can you be more specific? What do I think of what?" I asked, fake-smiling at Mary after she placed our glasses in front of us. She sat and sipped some wine she'd poured into her own, and I raised my eyebrow. She did, too.

That little shit.

"If he was killed for beating that woman, do you think it was right?" Tasha said.

We were on dangerous ground, not because I was going to tell Tasha anything about Jefferson Dobson, but because I didn't know how honest I should be. I liked and respected her very much and wanted to be truthful. But if she ever suspected me, I knew what would happen.

"Did they think he might kill her someday? If so, were they going to do anything about it before he did?"

Mary sipped her wine and looked back and forth between Tasha and me like she was watching a tennis match, smiling when I caught her eye.

I wondered if she knew about Dobson.

"Does it matter?" Tasha asked.

"It might be the reason he was killed – to save her life. But, if he was killed solely for beating her with impunity, then yes, it was the right thing to do. That woman shouldn't have to suffer because the police, or the courts, couldn't protect her."

Mary stopped moving her head and stared at me. So did Tasha. I guess I'd opted for a high degree of honesty.

"Why not just beat him up? Teach him a lesson that way?" Tasha said.

"Because men who beat women don't change and won't be rehabilitated. After he healed up, he'd continue to beat her, maybe to death. So the question becomes, do you give him a chance to change or give her a chance to live?"

"You think that's appropriate punishment for beating someone? To kill them?" she asked, concerned.

I should stop. Really.

"In this case, yes. He'd had his chances. And he needed to die so she could have hers."

Maybe it was how I'd said it, the certainty of my words, or the tone of my voice. Whatever it was, Tasha looked at me differently.

"Which is precisely why people like me shouldn't be in the vigilante business. Like I said earlier, it's difficult to find the *fair and right* between the neighbor's dog and the murdered child. Punishment in the eye of the beholder is tricky," I said with a smile, inviting them to join me.

Mary gave a grin, but Tasha didn't. She just watched me drink my rootbeer and rock in the big chair.

Tasha had never seen this side of Dax. The manner in which he was making a case for murder was disconcerting, but the finality in his voice as he handed down his judgement was ice-cold.

It troubled her

She remembered when Dom first told her about Jefferson Dobson being killed in front of his ex-wife's house. He'd said Dobson had beat her for years and somebody probably said 'enough.'

Isn't that what Dax just said? With calm conviction?

Could he have killed that man?

The cop in her felt something in her gut, but the friend in her didn't know how the cop could consider such a thing. How could she even think it?

She sipped her wine as they both joked around and felt apart from them for the first time since she'd found Mary. It made her sad and lonely. She couldn't lose them but didn't know if she could let it go.

"Dax? If I ask you a serious question, will you tell me a serious truth?"

I was afraid I'd have to look into her eyes and stone-cold lie to her, and my heart began to break. It felt like a genuine betrayal, and I realized she meant more to me than I'd thought.

"Well," I said, nodding my head toward Mary, "if you were *this* one, the truth would be guar-an-teed."

Mary and I smiled. Tasha not so much.

"You're important to me, Tash. Truly. But without knowing what you'll ask, the best I can do is give serious consideration to telling you a serious truth."

Tasha marveled at the strange situation. Was she really going to ask Dax if he killed someone with an icepick? That was insane.

Then don't ask.

She remembered what Mary told her about their honesty, how they didn't ask questions unless they wanted to hear the truth. Did she want to hear it?

Already she'd worked herself into a dilemma, wanting to satisfy her curiosity but not trusting the response she'd be given. And it would ruin their friendship if she thought Dax was lying to her, not to mention making him a suspect.

She loved this made-for-each-other family and was a part of it now. Could she leave it because of an unsupported suspicion or be turned away by asking if Dax was a killer?

But what if he was*?*

Dax raised his brow, and Tasha asked her question.

"I only saw one piece of strawberry cheesecake in the refrigerator. Do you mind if I have it?"

I grinned, relieved I wouldn't have to lie and turned to Mary who looked at ease as well.

"Would you get that cheesecake for Tasha, please?"

Mary started to get up and Tasha stopped her.

"I can get it."

"No, Mary would love to be your serving wench. It'll help burn off those second-glass wine calories."

"I thought you'd forgotten that," she said

"Not even a little bit."

Mary stuck out her tongue and left for the kitchen.

As Tasha laughed, I gave her some thought.

Her interest in Dobson was a serious complication. Even more so because of my strong feelings for her. I didn't know if she knew anything or was just curious about my vigilante point of view, but I'd have to tread lightly for a bit.

Which meant my trip to Georgia would have to wait. Sara's mother had recently been paroled, and I wanted to have a chat with her, a violent chat. I'd have to be careful, though. Much carefuller than I'd been with Mr. Dobson. I know that's not a real word, but it was accurate.

After Mary put a placemat on the table, she gave Tasha the plate, sat in her spot against the soft arm of the couch, and cradled a soda. She raised her glass and grinned. I tipped back, remembering our first night together.

We'd come a long way.

"Hey, Tash. Would you play *Summertime* when you're done eating your cheesecake? The one you're not sharing, by the way."

"Mmmm, good," she said and took another bite.

Tasha nodded her head and reminded me of my attempt to highjack the song by over-playing the solo, causing all of us to break into laughter.

"He does get greedy come solo time," Mary said.

"Well, you won't have to worry about that tonight. I'll be lucky to strum the chords."

I moved my left arm around and tweaked the pain in my back. The Destin trip had aggravated it. Not my time alone with Tommy and Brenda, but the long drive to and fro.

"Do you remember that sweet little lead-in you played before the beginning of the song? It was so beautiful."

They both looked at me and fell out.

"What? Why are you laughing?"

I must have tickled their funny bone somehow because they were saying it to each other and cracking up.

"It was soooo beautiful," Mary said, pretending to swoon, and Tasha joined in with her own rendition.

"It was so beeaauuutifull."

"Well . . . it was," I said with an expression of rapture, making them laugh all over again.

A few minutes later when the girls stopped making fun of me, Tasha said it was the sound of the Martin that inspired the melody she'd played.

"You talk about something being beautiful. The tone and timbre of the strings could bring tears to a deaf man. It can be felt in the heart and make your soul sing."

We nodded, Mary and I, appreciating the poetry of her feelings. We liked her a lot.

"That's a great guitar you have, Dax."

"It's not his, it's mine. It was the last good thing my dad gave me before he . . ." Mary said, and got quiet.

Tasha probably thought she'd had a painful memory, but I knew differently.

To her credit, Mary didn't look over at me.

Tasha nodded and then remembered something lost and forgotten, if it had ever really been known, about a guitar not being where it was.

"When did you get it? I'm assuming you didn't take it with you the night you walked to the forest, right? The night Dax found you."

"No, of course not. It was some night after that."

It looked like it was settled until I saw Tasha's eyes. Something wasn't right, and she asked another question.

"Do you know when that was?"

Mary did a good job of remaining calm. "Not really. Shortly after I left, but long before you found me."

Tasha nodded her head and asked another.

"Do you remember telling me you didn't go back? You said you hadn't seen your father or gone back to the house since that night. Remember?"

I would have to intervene in another minute to take the pressure off of Mary.

"Yes. I must have forgotten about going when I told you that. Probably didn't seem important. It's not, is it?"

I had to give it to her; Mary was handling herself well. She was cool under fire.

"Dax, did you go with her when she got her guitar?"

"Yes. We used her key to get into the house, making sure her father wasn't home by looking in the garage first for his truck." I liked to use the truth whenever possible. Especially when being questioned by the police.

"Do you know when that was? How long after you found Mary in the woods?"

"What does it matter now?"

"Please. Just tell me."

I thought about pulling out a coin and flipping it to see who'd answer first, but Tasha didn't seem like she was in a playful mood. She looked serious. Detectively.

The best way to proceed was to answer her question with a small, white lie. One I could live with.

"Tasha, I don't know why this is starting to feel like an interrogation, but I trust you're going to tell us. I think we got the guitar five or six weeks after I found Mary. After the papers said they'd disappeared, and after we thought it was safe to go."

That didn't sit well with her and she told us why.

"After the two of you went missing, I searched her house for bodies or explanations. I looked in every room and didn't see a guitar anywhere. I *did* see it on one of the videos from the flash-drive. It was standing up in the corner by the couch," she said, looking from me to Mary to me. "Can you explain that?"

I could but wasn't going to.   Instead, I tried to
undermine her belief in what she thought she didn't see.

"Is it possible your mistaken? You weren't specifically
looking for a guitar, so why are you so certain you didn't see
one? I mean, do you remember how many pairs of shoes
were in the hallway by the garage door, or what color the
shower curtain was in the bathroom?"

I hated to belittle her memory this way, trying to cast
doubt on her ability to recall what she'd seen on a day
almost a year ago. It didn't feel right, but it had to be done.

Tasha looked miffed.

"There were five pairs of shoes on a rug that probably
held seven. One pair was missing between the first and
third pairs, and another pair could have fit easily outside the
sixth," she said and continued.

"The shower curtain had white and yellow daisies
against a blue sky. There were also daisies on the floor of
the bathtub to prevent slipping."

I looked over at Mary who nodded and smiled. I
couldn't keep from grinning myself and told Tasha it was an
impressive display of recollection.

She cracked a little smile and the tension lightened for
a moment before I played my last card.

"Still, you could have just missed it. Did you take
pictures or video while you were in the house?"

Tasha shook her head, and I thought I'd planted a seed
of doubt. I didn't want to tear her down but couldn't explain
why it wasn't there any other way.

She'd have to take the hit.

"No. If it were a crime scene, we'd have plenty, but this
was just a look-see for evidence of foul play."

There it was. Reasonable doubt.

"But I didn't need a camera. I have an eidetic memory."

Well, shit. And how cool is that?

"You mean a photographic memory?"

"No one really has a photographic memory," Mary said.
"You can't just take a picture with your mind. An eidetic
memory can, however, recall images even after only a short
period of exposure. Vividly and accurately."

She looked over with empathy and tenderness and said, "Oh, Tasha. I'm so sorry,. Those dreams . . ."

I didn't know what they were talking about, but I couldn't waste time wondering about it. I needed to explain a missing guitar to someone who didn't miss much and didn't forget anything.

"Tash, is it at all possible you just didn't see it? It's the only thing I can think of."

And it was. I couldn't find a way to dispel her suspicion, even though she'd never be able to verify it. Unless she hadn't erased the videos on that drive.

"No," she said. "I looked everywhere."

"Did you look under the bed?" Mary asked,, and Tasha and I both looked at her.

"Under my bed. Did you look there?" she asked again.

I glanced over to Tasha who shook her head.

"No, I didn't. Huh. Why didn't I?" she said, confused.

"Why would you? What would you be looking for? There was barely enough room to fit my guitar case. And unless you smelled decomposition in the room, you wouldn't have any other reason to think to look."

Tasha gave Mary a smile.

She's sharp. And she's right. Why would anyone look under a bed only ten inches from the floor if there wasn't a compelling reason?

"Guess that answers that," I said, hoping like hell it did.

Tasha nodded.

'Thank God,' she said to herself, though she didn't really believe in one. She had started to worry Dax, maybe even Mary, had something to do with her father's disappearance.

Which wouldn't have crossed her mind if she hadn't already wondered if he'd killed a man who beat his ex-wife. If Dax could do that, what would he do to someone who raped their child?

What would *I* do? she thought. Tasha decided to give the question more consideration. Another time, though. She wanted to play and sing and be with her friends.

Her family.

As Tasha played that beautiful lead-in to *Summertime*, I looked at Mary and raised my eyebrow, asking if her guitar was ever under the bed. She grinned and shook her head.
I love that little girl.

thanks for reading

I imagine only five or six people will buy and read this book: my children and my best friend. Unfortunately for them, they're obliged to do so. Hopefully, they'll understand why I made them pay full price – so I can justify having a book signing party.

For those of you not so obligated, I hope you've enjoyed this first attempt of mine. I sure had fun writing it. Maybe you had some, too.

Thank you for spending your time with me.

larehalebooks@gmail.com

something to ponder

excerpt from **Let God Do His Own Killing**.

I'm always troubled when I hear of people killing in the name of God, or Allah, or whatever deity needs a school bus full of children blown up or a little ethnic cleansing.

I was raised in a Christian environment, reading a King James version of the Bible, and the awesome might and power of God is both documented and illustrated therein.

He flooded the world, destroying everyone save the inhabitants of the Ark. And when the wickedness of Sodom and Gomorrah could no longer be tolerated, He obliterated those cities in an instant. And on and on and on.

Now, I'm not questioning His righteousness, just acknowledging His capability and willingness to kill.

So, why do some think He needs us to help Him with that? Or wants us to?

If you accept the omnipotence of whatever Being you pray to, the question becomes . . . Why would He ask any of us to kill anyone but allow a Hitler to live? Or Pol Pot? Stalin, Saddam, Mladic', Mao?

Lucifer?

If your God can't reach down and kill your enemies for you, well, there you are. If He won't, then pray. Maybe He has His reasons. Just stop saying Allah wants this Jihad, or God wants that Crusade.

Because it's a lie.

People who kill in His name are killing for themselves, and those who believe otherwise are delusional.

'God moves in mysterious ways,' is often the reply given when a reason is sought but instead met with silence.

I don't understand why He allows evil in the world, and maybe I'm not meant to. But if God wants those kids blown up, let him do it himself.

when murder becomes mayhem

"Dude. You know there's a bathroom in the house, right? I mean, there are three of them. Why are you always going outside to pee?"

"It's a call of the wild, thing. Only, in this case, I'm the *wild thing* being called. I gotta go where I gotta go, and man, I gotta *go*." Troy turned and headed for the door.

"Hell, man, we ain't waitin.' That girl's raring to go. She's been giving it away ever since we made her a *star*."

A friend of theirs was a chemist, a gifted one, and he'd created a drug to lower the inhibition and raise the libido. They'd used it sparingly on a few girls, and its success had exceeded expectation.

Sex was now a plentiful bounty in the house.

"Yeah. A ruined reputation will do that, sometimes. When nobody believes you didn't do anything, you say *fuck it* and end up doing everything. And everybody," Troy said, and stepped outside into the backyard.

"Besides, you don't want me to go first. She's not gonna want any of y'all once I give it to her."

"Fuck you," Gregg called out, laughing his head off. "Let me know if it's *deep*, you freak of nature."

Troy chuckled as he walked away and raised his hand to give a backwards wave. The moon was bright enough to follow a trail over the dune and through the sawgrass, ending near a copse of trees by the water.

The dock was his favorite place to relieve himself. His stream sounded like a waterfall, and he'd imagine he could feel the bottom.

Gregg's comment came from an old joke about two guys peeing off a bridge into the river below arguing about who was bigger.

"Man. The water's cold."

"Yeah," his friend says. *"It's deep, too."*

To say Troy was well-endowed would be a significant understatement. At six-foot four, two-hundred thirty-five pounds, he was an impressive physical specimen. But it was his attribute that defined him. Friends on the baseball team said he was a double-threat at the plate – he could hit the ball out of the park with the bat in his hands or lay down a bunt with the one between his legs.

Troy was a good athlete and played many sports at the university, but the one at which he excelled was women. Troy could have anyone and gave to those who wanted him. And from those who didn't, he took.

Not like Gregg or some of his frat brothers. They'd slip something in a girl's drink, gang up on her, and then blackmail her into having sex with them afterward. It worked more often than not because the girls they captured on camera performed like *pornstars* and would do almost anything to keep it private, especially from their family.

No, he liked to take his women the old-fashioned way – by force. A girl who didn't want him revved his motor, and he set about putting her in a compromising position by whatever means necessary – charm, respect, and, most importantly, empathy. Validating a girl's feelings fostered her trust. Then the fun began.

He never spiked a drink or gave a girl any kind of drug. It just wasn't sporting. He might use a little alcohol to loosen her up but not enough to inhibit her ability to make an informed decision.

Troy was all about a woman's right to say no. He believed in it, supported it, and in fact preferred if she did – because taking a girl against her will was the high he craved. He'd then own her, and she'd know it for the rest of her life.

Of course, she might say it was rape, which it was. But it would be hard to prove because she'd be bruised and bloodied even if she gave herself freely. He was big, and most girls were not.

He'd raped more than thirty girls and had never been arrested though the police had spoken to him several times.

He was charismatic and believable. Also, being a star athlete at a major university meant the administration tended to protect their interests by maligning the victims.

Life was good, damned good for Troy who at nineteen had the world by the balls, and the girls by the . . .

He pulled himself free and took a wide stance, placed his fists on his hips and looked out at the dark. When the waterfall cascaded into the bay, he imagined himself the master of all he surveyed and closed his eyes.

It's deep, too.

A branch fell through the limbs of a tree to his right. Before it landed, an explosion of pain made him double-over. He instinctively reached between his legs and his ass was kicked into the water.

The tide was falling but he still had to stand to keep from drowning, which was difficult because the agony kept him hunched over. Someone jumped in after him, and he thought it might be one of his house brothers come to help. But when he peered through the pain, he saw who it was.

"You?" he said and fell backward when he stepped forward and slipped. He swallowed some water and started to cough then felt the arm tighten and started to choke.

"Yup. It's me," he heard from behind him.

He tried to stand but couldn't and was pushed under when he rolled to his knees. With herculean effort, he finally managed to lift his head from the water, but the stranglehold had become a death grip.

Troy slipped into a coma, unaware the arm had been released to repair some of the cellular damage to the exterior of the neck by letting the heart pump and circulate. He didn't feel the sharp slash of the pen shell or mind that his blood trailed behind the kayak as it towed him away.

And soon, after his lungs swapped out air for saltwater, he never minded about anything else ever again.